Going Coastal

Going Coastal

An Anthology of Lake Superior Short Stories

Lake Superior Writers

NORTH STAR PRESS OF ST. CLOUD, INC.
St. Cloud, Minnesota

ISBN: 978-1-68201-069-3

First edition: May 2017

Printed in the United States of America.

Published by
North Star Press
19485 Estes Road
Clearwater, MN 55320
www.northstarpress.com

Contents

Introduction

oing Coastal showcases the winning short stories from Lake Superior Writers' 2016 contest, which accepted entries from writers around Lake Superior.

Contest organizers requested fictional stories set in and around Lake Superior that describe its people, its history, folklore, environment, wildlife, businesses, communities, culture, or whatever moves writers about this place. Lake Superior was to be the main location for the stories, but other locations could be included.

The contest judges were Josh Bernstein, Marlais Brand, Marion Gustafson, Lacey Louwagie, Linda Olson, and Felicia Schneiderhan.

Purchase of this book supports Lake Superior Writers, a nonprofit organization located in Duluth, Minnesota, which fosters the artistic development of writers and a vibrant literary arts community in northeastern Minnesota and northern Wisconsin. To learn more, visit lakesuperiorwriters.org.

The Urge for
Going

Phil Fitzpatrick

Whispers.

We have been waiting for you.

An ageless wind rakes the gnarled bark and the branches above.

I know, Ahsinneeg, but who will keep the stories now?

A gentle rippling of the deeps below. Night darkening.

There is no need for worry. Someone will come, just as you came. It does not matter when someone comes. The stories will endure, just as we do.

Breathing more difficult now, but the whispers ease the pain.

Like us, they were born before memory and altered slowly by time. They lived within you while you lived, and you gave them breath. Quiet, now. We have a story for you.

Dying is part of the life of mortals, but it is not what rocks know.

Yes, it is good, then, good. I will rest now.

* * *

Cisco Two Feathers was driving home. Forty-two years of living in St. Paul had clouded most of the stories in his memory and had even erased others. It had not been enough to be volunteering in the Indian community; the children were more interested in their devices than in his stories. The parents were too busy to be interested in what he had to say. The older he got, the more frustrated he became, and on his seventieth birthday, he decided the only present he wanted was to go back home. Knowing that it would be impossible to recover any stories in St. Paul, he had left his job at the Minnesota Historical Society, his community, and the friendships he had formed since 1968. He wanted them back, the lost and even the partly obscured stories. More than that, he wanted to live where people still listened to them. He knew the only way to begin retrieving stories was to move back home to Grand Portage, but he also knew that neither the stories nor an audience were going to be easy to reclaim right away. He was heading toward an uncertain future three hundred miles away, toward a culture many years older; the move was an unsettling, if not a frightening prospect for a seventy-year-old man of the city. But the time was at hand.

Cisco was full-blooded Anishinaabe. In the old days, the days of his grandparents and before, his people were Ojibwe. Centuries before that, they were Chippewa. As a child, he had known many of their stories, stories of his family and their families, origin stories about The Beginning of all People. They were rich in colorful details, full of characters and situations that kept young ones and elders alike entertained and even spellbound for hours on long cold winter nights. They were always imaginatively told or sung in the annual way storytelling was done among the Anishinaabeg.

St. Paul

On Interstate 35E, the traffic was at a full stop at Maryland Avenue. Cisco looked out his window at the rearview mirror and gazed at the skyline, reminding himself that the First National Bank was now only the third tallest building in St. Paul. The blinking "1" had been there for as long as he could remember. Car trips all the way down Highway 61 into St. Paul in the late 1940s. The chemical smell hanging in the air as they drove between the buildings at 3M. The sturdy bulwark of the St. Paul Cathedral and the glistening gold horses on the State Capitol looming to the west. And the hypnotic red numeral "1" blinking above the First National Bank.

As a child, he had wished it had been a steady green and not an intermittent electric red. Staring at the single red numeral lent sadness to his sense of uncertainty and loss.

He took a last look at the sturdy old city he knew well as the line of cars began to creep forward again. He accelerated the truck slowly through the newly widened, freshly black-topped surface of Interstate 35E bedecked with orange cones and cement median barriers.

Cisco knew where he was going. The irregular but always memorable weekend trips back home had given him plenty of chances to memorize the asphalt pathway leading out of one century back toward an earlier one. He had planned for a few significant stops north of Duluth, knowing he would not be tempted by the many commercial diversions that had popped up over the years. He had had plenty of practice avoiding such diversions during his time in the Twin Cities.

The traffic in front of him continued to loosen now, and the late winter piles of dark chocolate slush moved past more quickly as he headed toward I-694. It was a depressing time of year, and he considered leaving the interstate and heading east to Highway 61 just to get away from the rush-hour press of people in a hurry. Once, he had known the need to hurry, but not anymore. What he was heading for and where it was located had not gone anywhere over the decades, and it certainly was not going anywhere anytime soon.

He disliked interstate travel. Too fast and too reckless. By the time he was approaching Forest Lake, he decided to leave I-35 and finish his trip on Highway 61. Turning right at the top of the exit ramp, what he saw made him think he could have been in any big city in the country. KFC and DQ, Taco Bell and Subway, Holiday stations on both sides of the street, Kwik Trip and Super America. And St. Paul-style traffic.

Chuckling at the irony of "Super America," he returned to I-35, staying in the exit lane connecting to Highway 8. Moving smoothly eastward toward 61, he breathed a sigh of relief. It would not be long now before he would feel the haze and clamor of the metro area vanish, releasing his spirit. The gray skies and blustery winds did their best to weigh him down, but Cisco felt lighter by the mile. He knew he was exactly where he was supposed to be, doing exactly what he was supposed to do. He knew there would be new challenges to face and new burdens to bear, but he knew he was well-equipped to cope with whatever changes awaited him.

As he usually did on his return trips, at Black Bear Casino just outside Carlton, Cisco turned back to the interstate so he could cruise slowly down Thompson Hill with the lift bridge in the distance, that metallic rectangular frown arching up over Canal Park in Duluth.

The other reason for returning to the interstate was so he could get through the city without being disappointed once again by the inability of the city's old face to have any kind of permanence. Restaurants, jewelers, hospitals, car dealerships, and billboards blaring the existence of these modern businesses now owned the city that once belonged to railroads, tankers, fishing boats, brownstones, and bungalows. Luckily, there was still Park Point; Cisco remembered stopping on occasion to walk its sandy shores collecting beach glass and agates. Today, however, he just wanted to return to Highway 61, or "Old Highway 61," as it was now appropriately but affectionately named.

Stoney Point

North of Duluth, on the uneven drive up Old 61, time tended to stand fairly still, measured only by an infinity of water and sky. Sometimes, the shoreline contributed to the picture when the dead and dying birch trees opened out to the deltas at Split Rock or Gooseberry or any one of the dozens of other rivers and streams along the North Shore that fed into the great lake. The faded yellow lines that bisected the aging blacktop were split by widening cracks, telling a simple story of wintry decades and diminished care. Occasional real estate signs on both sides of the highway were the primary barometers of change, along with new convenience stores and fast food restaurants.

While Cisco had lost many of his grandfather's stories, he still clearly remembered all the sights and sounds of the Lake Superior shoreline. One of the most dramatic had been the pounding of wind-driven waves at Stoney Point, where Grandfather would stop on the way down to or back from St. Paul. Sometimes he would park there for almost an hour with the engine running and the window cracked so they could hear the sound of huge waves whooshing up through the basalt platforms at the shore. On those visits, Grandfather's soothing voice was the complete opposite of the crash of the waves.

Those geysers are like my stories. The wind breathes life into them just like I breathe life into the stories. One day you will do the same thing, little Cisco.

Sometimes the spray came almost to the road, and the boy would feel a fine mist sneak through the open window.

I'm cold, Grandfather. Can we go now?

It wasn't so much the cold as it was the smoke from Grandfather's cigarettes. He loved hearing Grandfather's voice, but he usually started feeling sick after the second or third story. He would roll his window down a little farther to get more air in the back seat, and then he would get colder.

Yes, we will go. It is still winter, all right. Chinoodin will be here for many more days. We will stop again on the way home.

There were houses on St. Louis County 222, now called Stoney Point Road, but Cisco remembered when only a few fishing shacks and old boat shells dotted the road. In those days, people went to Stoney Point to fish or camp, as well as just to visit the lake, but no one lived there and certainly not in winter. On their way back home, Grandfather would stop again, and Cisco would listen to a few more stories, always with the background of the lake wind driving the waves onto the rocky shore. He used to wonder how these rocks could put up with this beating for so long.

These rocks are stronger than any Chinoodin, Grandson. Why do you think the wind spends so much time trying to break them apart?

Cisco now pulled off North Shore Drive and onto the dirt road leading down to the shore at Stoney Point. He saw a "For Sale" sign in the driveway of one of the smaller houses set back and up a hill. *How nice it would be to live here*, he thought, but he knew it would not feel like home. He drove along until he reached the opening where he and Grandfather used to stop. The day was lively with clouds and the sound of the offshore wind. The waves splashed onto the basalt platforms just as they had always done. *So much time has passed, and Chinoodin still tries to be stronger than the rocks*, Cisco thought, smiling and watching for a few more minutes. He rolled the window down and listened.

We are Ahsinneeg. We are still the strongest. We are not bothered by your noisy howling, Chinoodin, or by your vain and ceaseless pounding.

The sky was beginning to take on a warm afternoon glow, and the air was getting colder. Cisco knew it was time to get back onto the highway and head toward Two Harbors. There were many places he wanted to stop, but he did not want to arrive in Grand Portage too late. Beth would not want to stay awake much past nine o'clock. Knowing his ways when driving along Lake Superior, she had made him promise he would arrive by then. He would have to pass up Agate Bay and Split Rock. At this point, stopping at Lockport for coffee and a short visit was all he would have time for before reaching Grand Marais.

Ziibi, maybe there will be time for one of you. Maybe Temperance or Baptism or one of the gentler ones like Crow Creek or Wood's Creek. We will see.

The days when Grandfather would coax Cisco and Beth into the car for the drive south seemed so far away now, and it was embarrassing when Beth would ask him to tell her grandchildren a story. He would struggle to remember even one. Moving to St. Paul by itself should not have erased the stories, he would often tell himself, but there were other stories now. Many new stories had covered up the old ones, stories of people he had met and friends he had made. There were stories he had seen at the Uptown and the Lagoon theaters in Minneapolis. Movies were stories, too, and he remembered many of them. His friend Chris Spotted Eagle had taught him about making movies, and at one time, he had wanted to work for Spotted Eagle Productions. Soon enough, though, he realized that this was not his purpose. *Teach people, especially the young ones,* he kept telling himself. *That is what your true calling is.*

He clicked the seat belt mechanically and pulled slowly away, still watching the surf pounding on the rocks of Stoney Point. The spray became indistinguishable in the rearview mirror as he turned up and away from the lake. He felt numbed by the chill and the hypnotic effect of remembering Grandfather. The man who had given him and Beth a new life more than sixty years ago had long since passed on, but he certainly had not disappeared like so many of his stories now had. Scarcely a day went by that Cisco did not remember some phrase, some words of wisdom, or some wry bit of humor from the man who raised his two grandchildren, Beth and Cisco, by himself.

Travel far, little Cisco, but be sure in your heart never to leave home.

Two Harbors

Knife River was empty. The restaurant once known as Emily's that he used to dream of owning was closed. A large yellow "For Sale" sign hung from a metal post in the yard now. *Time and misfortune continue to catch up to this place,* he thought. He wanted to drive down to the marina and look at the boats, but it was getting late. Some other day, maybe, when the owners had started putting their big sailboats with the strange names back in the water. *Frigate Bird; I Owe, I Owe; Lady of the Lake,* and the Indian ones, *Nokomis; Gitchi Manito;* and *Sacajawea.* There were the disrespectful ones, too, like *Poke & Haunt Us* and *Sioux Bee.*

Grandfather had done his very best to educate his two impressionable grandchildren about disrespect and what one could and could not do about it. Cisco knew it involved much more than the "sticks and stones" lessons his teachers had used to try to calm him down at the Indian boarding school in Pipestone. He sometimes forgot about Grandfather's advice.

When people say bad things to you, it means they do not know how to rid themselves of the badness that lives inside them. Feel sorry for them, and do not let their badness become a part of your life even though it hurts.

Not having time to visit Agate Bay disappointed Cisco. He always felt warmly toward the three giant, deep brown ore docks that loomed above the bay. Looking at them from the opposite side, they reminded him of three legs of an invisible sphinx up in the clouds. He used to imagine being at the end of one of them and jumping off into the deep blue of Agate Bay. Now, he wished he could just walk out to the end of the breakwater below the lighthouse. He had no idea when he would be back down this far, but he knew it would not be soon. Gradually resuming his speed, he remembered another one of Grandfather's lessons.

When you are calm, Trouble gets frustrated, and sooner or later, he will leave you. When you are calm and alert, you see things others do not see, whether or not Trouble is still around.

Trouble became practically a brother when Cisco was little, and it got worse at Pipestone. If it had not been for Beth, he did not know how he would have coped with the disappearance of his father, then the death of his mother, and finally the long trip down to Pipestone to go to the Indian school. It had felt like an eternity before Grandfather finally arrived to pick them up after the school closed in 1953.

You have been away from home long enough. There is work to be done, and I am getting old.

Grandfather always sounded more stern than he really was. As happy as Cisco and Beth both were when they were once again reunited with their grandfather in Grand Portage, they knew that he was even happier, and Cisco remembered every one of the joyful stops Grandfather had made on the way home.

He turned the radio on now in hopes of getting the signal from WTIP in Grand Marais. It usually came in clearly after he passed through the Silver Creek Cliff tunnel. By the time he reached Palisade Head, Cisco was getting sleepy in spite of the music. There were still three stops to make, not counting any he would make on the spur of the moment. But Palisade Head, with its craggy rhyolite bluffs and spectacular view of the lake, was a must for any person of the lake returning home after being gone so long.

Grandfather used to tell him that there was no better view of Gichigami than the one from Palisade Head. *Remember it well,* he would say; Cisco found it easy to follow his grandfather's advice. During the four years in Pipestone, it was one of the things he could picture clearly that prevented sadness from staying too long with him. He used to have to remind Beth to do the same, although school was much easier for her. His older sister just had a way about her, a way that seemed to keep loneliness and trouble at a distance. Even after he had moved to St. Paul and found his way to the Indian community there, Beth still urged him to return.

This is your true home, Nishiime. Why do you not believe this? My children want you here. I want you here. We are your family.

Cisco knew his older sister spoke from her heart. She always had. When the Indian officials had come to Grand

Portage to take them to Pipestone, there was more sadness in the household than he or their grandfather could handle, more sadness even than after their parents were gone. But Beth somehow managed to rise above the sadness and tell both her brother and Grandfather that it was all right, that time would bring them back together again, that she would look after her younger brother. And she did.

Nishiime, you must not speak to these people without thinking! Nishiime, you must study and think about these lessons now because they will help you in both worlds! Nishiime, you must learn when to speak up and when to stay silent!

Beth was a good sister. He owed her more than he knew how to repay after so many years of advice and generosity, friendship, and love. Her beauty was much deeper than just what she looked like, but when she had married Travis a few years after they had returned from Pipestone, Cisco found himself feeling possessive of her attention. It felt like another loss, and became one more reason for moving to St. Paul. Standing at the edge of Palisade Head now and looking out over the vastness of Lake Superior, Cisco felt two kinds of warmth. There was the warmth of this ageless panorama before him, one he had known since childhood. And there was the warmth that came from knowing he was going home and would be welcomed back into the embrace of his sister, her grandchildren, the entire community, and the memories and stories they shared.

Far out in the lake, Cisco spotted one of the season's early ore boats churning out into the wider, more open water. Many times in years past, he had watched these gigantic vessels and their proud pilot houses with smoke pluming behind them. As a child, he had wished to be the pilot of one of those boats, but when he told his grandfather of his dream, he simply replied there were many dreams far less dangerous to pursue.

Gichigami has a short temper, Little One, and you never know when her tantrums will come. She does not care whom she frightens, whom she injures, or whom she drowns.

The wind was increasing, and it was getting colder. Cisco hurried back to the truck and descended to the highway. He was worried about getting to Beth's home by nine o'clock, when he knew she would be getting ready for bed. The grandchildren would arrive the next day, and both he and Beth would need a good night's sleep in preparation. He had felt something catch in his chest as he was climbing up into the truck but assumed it was just gas or maybe a pulled muscle from hoisting himself up into the cab several times already that day.

He was sorry not to be able to stop at Shovel Point, remembering how fond Grandfather was of taking his grandchildren to the campground for a weekend trip long before the area had become a state park. They would camp right at the shore, and Grandfather would make a chicken-and-rice stew. The best part of those trips was the campfire and the stories of Grandfather's childhood in Grand Portage. On one trip, when they were still very young, Beth and Cisco asked him where Grandmother was. They had been wondering about this for a long time, but they could not summon the courage to ask him. That campfire was somehow the right time, they agreed. After a long silence broken only by the crackling of the fire and an occasional barred owl's hooting, Grandfather told them their Grandmother had been with Gichi manidoo since before they were born.

Your grandmother was so beautiful and such a loving mother and so trusted a friend that Gichi manidoo came to me one night and asked me if he could have permission to carry her away. He wanted her to help him with all the lonely and unhappy souls in the Dream Time.

That was all he said. After his explanation, they thought even more reverently about their grandmother than they had before, and it was never a source of curiosity again.

Cisco left Illgen City in the fading sunlight. He knew it would be dark before he reached Grand Marais, but there was no way he could skip the remaining stops. The Temperance River would bring back a fresh collection of Grandfather memories, or perhaps a surprise location would appear. Then a cup of coffee at Lockport and on to Grand Marais. He guessed he would be on Beth's doorstep by 9:30. *I will only stay for a moment at one of the rivers,* he thought, knowing it would supply him with the needed energy for the rest of the trip.

Passing through Little Marais and Taconite Harbor and finally Schroeder, Cisco felt the firm and steady tug of the border country he had grown up in. It was a magnetism that had never left him, not in Pipestone and not in St. Paul. Now that he was less than one hundred miles from his home, the tug was getting more noticeable and more insistent. He thought about how angry he had been when the men came to take him to Pipestone.

But Grandfather, I don't want to go. I want to stay here. Why are they making us go? Where are they taking us? Can't you tell them we don't want to go to a different school?

Having to leave home as a ten-year-old was the hardest thing he could have imagined doing at the time. It made it worse that Grandfather told them he would drive the boy and his sister down himself. He remembered vividly that all the stops on the way down had been tainted by the fear he would never see his Grandfather again, never see home again. The ten-year-old imagination pictured a different world in a whole different part of the country with complete strangers, many rules, and no Gichigami. And all of that had been true.

Behind the dead and dying birches along the desolate stretch of highway between the state park and Schroeder, the great lake brooded. The gray-green water riffled gently by the late March winds looked as mysterious and powerful as ever. Impatient to be closer to the majestic waters, Cisco looked for an access point that was not a driveway. A few miles south of Little Marais, he saw another faded street sign reading "Old Highway 61." He slowed and veered off the new 61 onto the cracked, narrow, rust-colored two-lane road. He passed two mailboxes, one on each side, before coming to a dead end at fire marker 5966. Getting out of his truck, he heard the unmistakable sound of the lake breathing below him. He knew it would be impossible to climb all the way down, and even if he could, it would take too much time. It was enough just to stand in the thicket of stumps and saplings and feel the life of the lake drifting back into his soul. He remembered Grandfather taking him by the hand down through many different wooded places like this during those gentle years.

Listen, Cisco. This is the sound of your father and your mother. This is the sound of our people. Do you hear it, Grandson? Let Gichigami's breath fill you up so that it will stay with you until you come back. The lake has the breath of life within, and it will stay with you if you let it. Listen. Listen . . .

Cisco watched the vast lake waters below him roll slowly shoreward and listened to their unhurried collisions with the rocky beach. Today, there was no tempestuous spray or drastic suck back into the fullness. Just the endless breath Grandfather had taught him to listen for above the sounds of the highway and the chickadee chatter and the winds.

Looking back on those days now, it had turned out that leaving as a ten-year-old was not nearly as difficult for him as leaving home again eighteen years later had been. Once again, he was saying good-bye to people and places and a way of life he loved. After Beth and Travis got married, something he could not identify had changed inside, and moving to St. Paul seemed like the best option. Many of his friends had either enlisted or moved up to Thunder Bay to avoid the draft and Vietnam. The time and the people were different. Even Grandfather had seemed somehow restless on his grandson's behalf, anxious for him to go somewhere and begin a life that would be his own.

When he told Beth he was moving to St. Paul, she didn't understand. She was angry and said her children would certainly not understand either, that it would be especially hard on them. She had many questions for him for which he had no answers.

Brother, your niece and nephew love you so much, why are you doing this? Where will you stay? What will you do? Will you ever come back?

Leaving children behind as an adult was a quantum level harder than leaving adults as a child. Cisco remembered being tongue-tied trying to talk to his sister. He was not even certain he understood the whole situation himself, but he knew he had to go. He had often found himself singing Joni Mitchell's "Urge for Going" that year. He remembered liking the Tom Rush version better, but they were both good. He could not explain what it was about the song that stayed with him in those days.

And I get the urge for going when the meadow grass was turning brown.

Summertime is a-falling down, winter's closing in . . .

Grand Marais

Cisco had no idea what time it was, and the rock he had found to sit on looking out over the lake was getting uncomfortable. He had been there for a long time. He jumped up, suddenly remembering he had left the motor running in the truck. The sun was setting now, and the dead grass and dying birch trunks radiated yellow and gold. When he reached Lockport, he was almost out of gas. *Perfect timing,* he thought as he pulled in. Who would be working, Mabel or Louise? It never mattered; both of them were so welcoming and chatty that, after he'd had a meal or coffee or spent a few minutes looking around, he did not want to leave. He had first met them on his move south. In a rush to break away from home, he thought he was only stopping for gas that day. Two hours later, he had nearly decided to stay and be their groundskeeper. They called each other Mayb and Weezy. Mayb had said he would always be welcome, that they'd have a job for him whenever he wanted one. On his infrequent trips back home to visit over the years, he would plan his arrival to be no later than noon so he could enjoy breakfast with them.

After gassing up and asking Weezy for one of her best espressos, Cisco's truck lumbered back onto 61. He had two stops to make once he got to Grand Marais, each one requiring a half-hour. First, he would walk out to Artists' Point, and then make a brief stop at Edna Lewis's house. Edna would be glad to see him and would want to give him some soup, some crackers, and some advice. That was her way: simple, generous, and thoughtful with wisdom befitting her years. Cisco had been in love with Edna's daughter Yvonne from the time when Grandfather would drive him and Beth down to the Raspberry Festival in July and stretching through the years when she was in college in Minneapolis. That was why Grand Marais had always been as hallowed a place for Cisco as Grand Portage.

Darkness had begun to surround the lakeshore by the time he reached Terrace Point, with its panoramic view across Good Harbor Bay to the glittering lights of Grand Marais. He was only half an hour behind schedule, but it did not matter. He called Beth when he got into town, then parked the truck and began the easy walk out to the rocky perimeters of Artists' Point. Short though his time was out on this maze of volcanic outcroppings, it was an important pause in the journey. Cisco had the darkening ledges to himself, and he listened intently to the lullaby of the waves as they eased up onto the shelf and then receded to make way for the ones that followed. The memory of sitting in silence next to Yvonne and under a sky full of stars was as vivid as ever.

By 7:45, Cisco was at Edna's front door. She greeted him warmly, the familiar hug and wordless welcome lasting several minutes on the front porch. In spite of her many wrinkles and snow-white hair, in many ways she looked as youthful as when he first met her. Cisco beamed as Edna's saintly smile and twinkling eyes ushered him into her living room. How had these two outlived so many others and looked like such youngsters after countless reunions and stories both lengthy and brief? Cisco's questions about Yvonne followed by her questions about Beth and her grandchildren could easily have lasted for hours.

Turning down Edna's homemade soup was the only way Cisco could shorten the evening visit. After he promised to return frequently now that he had come home, and agreeing to take a quart jar of soup up to Beth, Edna gave him permission to complete his journey. His vow to return soon firmly locked in her memory and sealed with a parting embrace, she closed the door quietly and moved over to watch and wave at the front window. *In the next world*, Cisco thought as he climbed into the truck once more, *maybe I will be with her; it is probably too late in this one.*

Home

Chippewa City. Croftville. Red Cliff. Covill. Judge Magney State Park. Hovland. Red Rock. Finally, the Grand Portage National Monument and the casino. The last thirty-seven miles between Minnesota's capitol city and the historic fur trade town of Grand Portage just six and a half miles inside the Canadian border seemed as long as the initial two-hundred-sixty-mile drive to Grand Marais, and darkness made the distance seem even longer.

The time it took the carrier of a people's stories and a family's memories to return to his origins, however, was often over in little more than a single heartbeat, and the welcome did not wear out no matter how long the return lasted. The only thing that remained was for the stories and the memories to be recovered and then passed on to new carriers.

Cisco moved into Beth's old bedroom. After Travis had passed away, Beth moved downstairs into the den so she would have television in her bedroom. Gale's old room now doubled as her studio and the guest room. It was not long before Beth's neighbors began sending their children and grandchildren over to listen to Cisco Two Feathers talk to them about life in the big city or the importance of eating vegetables or how to whittle.

Cisco also started talking to some of the band members at the National Monument Headquarters about going out to Hat Point. He knew that years ago there had been enough damage to the Spirit Tree from vandals that the tribe had decided to require all visitors to be accompanied by a member of the band. As a child,

Cisco remembered Grandfather taking them out to see Manido gizhigans at least once every season. He would place a bag of tobacco near the base as an offering. One year it accidentally fell into the crack in the rock where the main root came out. Grandfather made a joke about it and said that Gichi manidoo always has a sense of humor about humans.

Gichi manidoo will be glad the tobacco is now safe from any greedy hands.

After settling in and getting used to being home, Cisco started looking for work. Of course, the community wanted him to start teaching school. Ojibwe language, cultural studies, tutoring; they would have been happy just to have him working in the school's kitchen. *You bring wisdom and experience*, the school officials told him. There were plenty of elders in the community who were wise, but they were appealing to his sense of pride and his generosity, and they told him no one had spent time in the white man's world as he had.

Flattered though he was, Cisco believed a full-time teaching position would be bad for his health, bad for Beth, and bad for her grandchildren. He was relieved that he knew how to say no, and he reassured the people at the school he would be available for substitute teaching, for lessons on Ojibwe language, and for special programs on Anishinaabe culture.

It was after he had started accompanying tourists out to Hat Point and the Spirit Tree that he began experiencing more chest pains. Beth took him to the Cook County North Shore Hospital and Care Center in

Grand Marais. Dr. Nelson, who had been Beth's family doctor since Gale's high school years, told Cisco he needed to slow down. *You're not a spring chicken, Mr. Two Feathers,* he had said. Cisco's pride would not let him agree, but he reluctantly said he would start taking the medication Dr. Nelson prescribed as well as a daily aspirin.

In spite of her always positive outlook, Beth was worried. *You stay home and rest,* she kept telling him. But there were days when he just couldn't. The school needed him, the grandchildren needed him, and the tourists needed him. One day, he was walking out to the Spirit Tree with three women who were elementary school teachers. They had driven up from St. Paul that morning and would be driving back in the evening. When Cisco told them he had lived in St. Paul for most of his life, they were stunned and wanted to know where his home had been. He told them he had lived in the Selby-Dale community and worked at the Historical Society as an educator and interpreter. They were full of questions about the Spirit Tree and about Anishinaabe culture and history. *We want to teach our students about Native Americans,* they said, adding that they were reluctant to start for fear of doing it incorrectly. Cisco was the right person at the right time that day; they could barely get a word in themselves, he was so talkative.

You are doing the right thing. Never be afraid to teach another culture to children, but never be afraid to ask for help either. If you are inquisitive, your students will be inquisitive.

The stories Cisco had learned from Grandfather and those he told Beth's grandchildren were the same stories that countless visitors to Grand Portage took back home with them during the years he worked as a guide at Hat Point. In the winter months, as was the custom among the Anishinaabeg, he told Nanibouzou trickster stories that taught lessons and entertained. When the snow was gone, he told family stories he had learned over the years from Grandfather. Though at first he remembered only a few of them, after less than a year, and with constant prompting by his sister, the stories began to return. His favorite place to tell them was out on Hat Point at the Spirit Tree, and the monument staff often allowed him to go out to this sacred spot by himself. There, he would sit and listen to the wind in the wispy needles above, to the waters below lapping lazily against the ageless rocks, and to the voice of Grandfather.

This is where the true stories live. You have learned them, and lost them, and recovered them again. But here, with Ashinneeg, they have never been lost. Take more of them back with you each time you go home.

* * *

Settled into a familiar notch in the rocks with the whispers all about. Just the watery sighing below. The Spirit Tree darkening and the stars emerging behind its branches.

Ashinneeg is telling me a story again. It is good.

The night sky glistens and the gentle whispered stories continue.

END

Phil Fitzpatrick is a retired English teacher who lives in Duluth with his black rescue dog, also named Cisco. He guided canoe trips in the BWCAW in the 1960s, spent four years in the education department at the Minnesota Historical Society during the time of the Quincentennial, and has taught all ages of learners, preschool through adult. There are still boxes of his first and only publication, *A Beautiful Friendship: The Joy of Chasing Bogey Golf*, on his front porch.

The Painting

Evan Sasman

The first time I met Grace she was standing at an easel, a paintbrush in one hand and a paint palette in the other. The painting in progress was as interesting as the artist. They were as intertwined as art should be.

The artist, in her mid-eighties in the mid-1980s, with graying hair and a dark complexion, stood barely five feet tall. Her back was severely stooped, like someone who had carried a great weight throughout her life. Her given name was Grace, but she was known in this part of the country as the Popcorn Lady. This part of the country was the south shore of Lake Superior.

Grace's moniker came from years operating her popcorn wagon parked on the main street of Ashland, Wisconsin, during the 1930s and 1940s, when the city supported three thriving movie theaters. Grace located her wagon equal distance from the movie houses so patrons of each could buy a bag before entering the theater of their choice for whichever double feature was playing. The Popcorn Lady was well-suited for the job. Her diminutive stature matched the wagon's low ceiling.

I was an historian in a region where the past reached back to the ice ages, through hundreds of years of Native

American culture, and into the arrival of French fur trappers as early as the mid-1600s. Grace depicted her past in the acrylic painting on the easel. It was a specific day that she was trying to bring into focus.

Grace was the granddaughter of an Ojibway medicine woman, one of the last of the old ones who had learned her craft steeped in a culture that was still extant. The old medicine woman had singled out Grace to learn the same skills and carry on the traditions.

The painting on Grace's easel depicted an arc of Lake Superior's shoreline, viewed from a high bank, scattered trees surrounding the set, at a place where a river, partially frozen by winter's cold breath, flowed into the lake. An ice shelf had formed on the lake, yet where river met lake, open water jetted and eddied as it joined the Lake Superior watershed. Half of the warmer river water ran under the ice shelf while the rest ran over it, as far as it could, until it transformed into ice waves.

Grace had taken up painting late in life—through classes designed for seniors—in part because the opportunity had simply presented itself, and in part because she held in her subconscious mind a vision struggling to surface, demanding her attention.

A friend who volunteered with seniors, who also valued history, told me about Grace and had suggested I meet her. When I arrived at her small apartment in a seniors housing unit she took time to show me some of her paintings—a few hanging on the apartment walls, others on the floor leaning against the walls so the paint could rest undisturbed while drying. She described some of the paintings, where they had come from, and what they meant to her.

When she came to the painting on the easel, she had to pause. She stared at her newest painting for minutes. It seemed as much a mystery to her as it was to me.

First, I would need to know the story, she said. She offered me coffee and we sat in chairs by a small desk. She noticed my hand, my prosthetic limb, but her eyes didn't linger long. Nearly everyone did notice, given enough time. Some people were polite and didn't stare. Grace was polite.

With fresh coffee all around, she began her story. When she was a toddler, her grandmother had carried her on her back as she made her rounds through northern Wisconsin and Michigan's Upper Peninsula. She traveled from one Ojibway settlement to another administering medicine, the way a country doctor would travel a circuit from town to town, she said.

Her grandmother brought Grace with her because she had high hopes for the young girl and wanted her to learn about medicine, about the various herbs, the many spirits, and the way to see the world.

On the day depicted in the painting, Grace was about four years old. Yet she remembered the place as if she were standing there now. She closed her eyes to better see it in her memory.

When they arrived at the lakeshore, her grandmother stopped. She stared at the flowing waters as if she were studying them, reading them. Then, as if she saw something troubling, she changed direction, walking on a new heading with a quickened pace. After walking five or six miles, Grace reckoned, they came upon a homestead. Her grandmother began searching the place as if she knew what to expect. They found a girl, a young, blonde white girl about six years old. The girl had fallen and broken her leg. Is this what her grandmother had seen in the water, Grace wondered?

Her grandmother tended to the girl's broken leg and then, finding no adults at the farm, placed Grace on the ground, and the white girl on her back. She then turned back toward Odanah and the Bad River Reservation.

Grace's grandmother carried the girl on her back, and Grace had to walk behind her all the way back to the family's cabin in the woods. There, her grandmother continued to nurse the white girl back to health, then kept her there and raised her as a member of the family.

"I remember that so clearly because I had to walk from that day on. My grandmother had replaced me on her back, and I had to walk on my own from then on," she said. She was resentful. She was angry. She remembered it well, and her emotional pitch helped preserve the memory of that fateful day.

Of course, decades had passed, and Grace found herself reconstructing the events as if she was trying to deconstruct an incident that still plagued her, like a four-year-old residing in her subconscious demanding attention. The child in Grace would not be denied.

The older Grace understood all this and with this painting was trying to soothe and satisfy the child. But the older woman needed to understand, too. This was the key to a greater understanding of who she was and what had been her purpose in this life. She had to know, and she had to know soon, as though part of her understood that her internal timetable was running out.

She refreshed my coffee and then, like a good host, she asked about me. Who were my people?

Well, I was the son of a Lutheran minister and, like her, was supposed to follow in my father's footsteps.

She asked about my hand. A farm accident, I explained, when I was young. I had nearly died. But that was more than twenty years ago.

When my coffee was gone, my mind pulled me back to daily concerns. The busy-ness of my world pressed on me, and I had to take my leave. She invited me to return. I accepted. I understood. The painting was not finished yet.

A week passed before I went to visit Grace again. During that time, when I had moments to reflect, pieces of her story came back to me. In northern Wisconsin, reflective moments were frequent anyway, and I seldom let those opportunities get away unobserved. They might come when sitting atop a bluff, watching eagles soar below, or sitting by a waterfall while that white noise occupied the mind, or while sitting next to Lake Superior's shores, falling into the rhythm of incoming waves.

A tribal elder once told me we all have places that speak to us, places to meditate, sacred places, he said. The only requirement was that they be in the natural world and draw us to them. You find your place to sit, and wait, he told me. Within twenty minutes, or perhaps a little longer, you will slip into the spirit world, a timeless place where your questions and their answers reside together. You simply wait, and focus on your problem, and the answer will come to you.

Despite the decades that separated us, Grace and I shared similar experiences. We both had expectations placed on our shoulders. We were both supposed to follow a spiritual path. She would become a medicine woman, and I would become a minister. Yet neither of us did.

Yet another similarity came to mind. She had been supplanted on her grandmother's back by another child. I had my own sibling rivalry issues. When my baby brother was born, and the moment came for me to meet the newest family member, my mother had told me, I went into the bedroom and stood at the foot of her bed glaring at her malevolently. I wouldn't come any closer. It was as though I blamed her for replacing me.

I wondered if there were more shared experiences with Grace.

When I next visited her, I could see she had added detail to her painting. A tree had been fleshed out. White water, missing previously, flowed more turbulent and uncontained by the ice blanket.

I asked Grace a question that had come to my mind since my last visit. "Why did your grandmother choose you to follow in her footsteps?"

"It skipped a generation. My mother wasn't interested," she answered.

Her mother had fallen in love and married a white man. It wasn't the white man component that disqualified her. It was the "falling in love" part.

Her mother wasn't just in love. She was fully and completely in love.

"They say that the children of parents that much in love become orphans to that love," she said. "I can say, from personal experience, that it's true." Grace's grandmother took the metaphorical orphan under her wing.

Not that Grace blamed her mother. Grace loved her father, too. He was a Scotsman, a surveyor. He had come north to survey what was then uncharted territory. But it wasn't his surveying skills Grace most admired. It was his musical skills. He was a great fiddler, she said, and was much in demand because of it.

Grace imagined that her mother had fallen in love with him for the same reason.

But that made both parents too distracted to be devoted to her. So, her grandmother stepped into the breech. No one objected, and Grace's grandmother began carrying Grace on her back almost from the time she was an infant, as if the baby had been bequeathed to her for some higher purpose. Grace stayed on her grandmother's back until that day in the Upper Peninsula.

"But you didn't become a medicine woman . . ."

"No. I became a Lutheran."

My mind reeled. "What happened?" was all I could think to ask.

She had been perhaps nine, maybe ten years old when it happened. A typhus epidemic swept through the area. Many people became sick. Most died.

"In those days, when there was an epidemic, they set up what they called pest houses," she explained. "When you became sick, they took you to the pest house. That way you were quarantined and wouldn't spread it. It was illegal to take someone out of the pest house. They cared for you there but really it was a place for people to go to die."

Grace became sick. She was taken to the pest house to die. She was expected to die.

Her grandmother was away in the Upper Peninsula on her rounds when Grace became ill. "But she knew," Grace said. The old woman immediately stopped what she was doing, turned around, and returned to Odanah.

"No one told her. No one sent her word. She just knew," Grace said. When her grandmother reached Odanah, she didn't go to the cabin to find out the news or discuss the options with her family.

"She went straight to the pest house and took me out of there," Grace said, as if this was further proof that her grandmother had simply known that her granddaughter was facing a life-threatening illness.

That was in late February, Grace said. After that she didn't remember anything again until: "I remember waking up in a hollow place, a small earthen cave or the hollowed-out depression from a fallen tree, you know, when the tree topples and the roots are pulled from the earth. Sometimes that makes a hollowed-out place in the ground. I was covered in leaves and a warm wind was blowing a blanket that had been used to cover the one small opening. It was spring and I had survived," she said. But the disease had taken its toll. Her back was deformed and her growth stunted. But she had survived.

"I remember it so clearly. It was a red wool blanket—a Canadian Army blanket. The Canadian Army blankets were red. The U.S. Army blankets were yellow. The Canadian Army blankets were highly prized. No one wanted the yellow blankets. They made people sick."

Because she had been sick, and because she still had a long recovery ahead, she stopped traveling with her grandmother. Then, over time, no one expected the sickly girl to become a medicine woman.

That's what had happened to me, after the farm accident, I recalled. The expectations were gone. Instead, it was all about recoveries and therapies and getting back to something that resembled normal. Once I found my balance again, I told my parents I didn't want to be a minister anymore.

I left Grace to her painting to get back to my life. That's when thoughts about spiritual places came to mind. I went to my most sacred place—St. Peter's Dome and Morgan Falls. That's what the U.S. Forest Service call them. The Ojibway call it "the place where eagles gather." It is about twenty miles south of Chequamegon Bay in the Penokee Range and from the top, on a clear day, you can see the bay.

It was a climb to the top of the dome, a couple miles gradually upward and then a steep ascent near the top.

I had found it not long after my wife died. She died shortly after we moved to northern Wisconsin, from cancer. She was thirty years old. I was devastated. We were deeply and fully in love. I scattered her ashes at the top of St. Peter's Dome.

Grace had been married, too. She married a man from the Lutheran Church she joined. They had operated the popcorn wagon together.

My wife was raised a Lutheran but was mostly Air Force brat and part Cherokee. She had been exploring the Cherokee part of her life before she died. She was an artist, and one of the paintings she had completed before she died was the face of a Native American woman, looking upward and into the cosmos.

St. Peter's Dome was my sacred place. There I sat and waited. After twenty minutes, maybe a little longer, I would slip into the spirit world. Once I was in the spirit world, an animal would come to me, the elder had told me. It would have a message for me from the Creator. I would know the message from the kind of animal it was and from its behavior.

Two eagles appeared. I was up so high that they flew below me. They were hunting, going about the job of surviving. Then, suddenly, one eagle flew straight upward. I watched it until it disappeared into a cloud. The other eagle, though, continued its hunt.

I took it to mean that the eagles represented my late wife and me. Unexpectedly, one flew up into the heavens, as if depicting my wife's death. The other, however, continued to go about the business of living. That's what I had to do. Go on living.

I could see two more similarities between Grace and myself. There had been a trauma in both our lives at an early age. I nearly died in that farm accident, the way Grace had nearly died from illness. And then?

And then afterward my life was suddenly on a different path. Other peoples' expectations didn't matter anymore. I had fought so hard to stay alive that my life had a new value I hadn't realized before. I had taken ownership. I had to live it for myself now.

Maybe Grace had felt the same way.

And for the second thing . . . no, it wasn't a similarity. It was a polar opposite. While I was groomed to be a Lutheran minister, I walked away from that. What came to fill that space instead was the spirituality contained in nature, and the belief system most attached to that, Native American beliefs. I didn't go looking for them. They found me when I needed them, when I was mourning.

But I couldn't help but see the ironic shifts in our separate lives. Grace was supposed to be a medicine woman and became a Lutheran. I was supposed to be a Lutheran minister and instead gravitated toward Native American beliefs. Is the universe we live in that delicately balanced? Did one person on a definite journey have to change direction to open a door for someone else to change direction?

The next time I saw her, I asked Grace how she became a Lutheran.

"I saw an angel," she said.

"You what?"

She was a teenager, on her way to a party, dressed in a flounced skirt while she displayed the latest hairstyle, walking alone along an Ashland street. She reached a railroad overpass, walking beneath it, where it suddenly became dark and foreboding. That was the street; she pointed out and downward from her apartment window. You could see it from there, even the old, rusting railroad overpass.

Just then, so many years ago, two men came out of the shadows beneath that overpass and followed her. She felt terribly afraid, a young Native American woman walking alone on the street. She felt her life was in danger, for someone who knew what that felt like. She felt as alone as she had ever in her life.

She walked faster and they walked faster. She could hear their footsteps behind her. Then, just as she was about to run, someone appeared in front of her, walking toward her. He was dressed in ordinary clothes but there was a glow around him. When the two men following her saw him, they turned and walked way. She saw them go as she looked over her shoulder. When she looked again to the front, the angel was gone. It had come from nowhere and had returned there just as suddenly.

That's when she joined the Lutheran Church.

There were a lot of ways to discredit her story about the angel. It could have just been an ordinary man. The two rowdies might have just been cowards scared off by a sudden appearance of someone they hadn't anticipated.

"No," she said. "It was an angel." She knew it. She could see it.

I've known Native Americans who lived with a foot in two worlds, who would take in a sacred sweat one day and then communion the next.

In some ways, I've done the same. I've been to both. I sang in the church choir when I was barely able to walk and joined in sacred sweats.

If we are the sum of our experiences, then I would probably be about twenty-three percent Christian, fifteen percent Buddhist, twenty-five percent Jungian psychologist, while leaning toward Native American perspective twenty percent of the time . . . and the rest? Uncertainty.

At one time in her life, perhaps Grace had needed the protection that angel offered. But now, decades later and with her remaining days dwindling, she needed a different perspective.

I stood and peered at the painting still on her easel, as if I needed to slip into the spirit world to see whatever Grace was searching for. There was something here, but she couldn't see it.

"I think it's done," she announced with certainty. Then, with equal uncertainty, asked me, "Do you think it's done?"

I looked at it closely. This friendship with Grace offered a unique perspective. I had learned to view my life through different eyes. Before, I was self-centered enough to think that the path I followed was the only right and true path. But then I could see the only right and true path for each of us was the one we chose, trusting that we'd choose the direction we need.

"You're the only one who knows that, Grace."

I didn't see her again. Whatever it was we were supposed to learn from each other was done, it seemed.

But I don't think the painting was, not when I last saw it, not quite. I think it took another three weeks for Grace to finish it. That's how long it was before she died. Knowing Grace the way I did, I don't think she would have gone until she had seen that river the way her grandmother had seen it.

END

Evan Sasman became a writer when he nearly died in a farm accident at age twelve. He discovered he had a lot to express and needed a way to express it.

He began by writing poetry and published a handful of poems in high school anthologies. He went on to a career in journalism and was recognized by the Wisconsin Newspaper Association with awards for Best Feature Story and Best Investigative News Story. He has often written about Native American issues. He worked for the Bad River Band, Lake Superior Ojibway Tribe for ten years as a teacher and journalist. "The Painting" is based on Ojibway culture. His book, *Equilibrium*, is a work of fiction based on the 1996 Ojibway railroad blockade on the Bad River Reservation in Wisconsin.

His late wife's ashes are scattered in the Chequamegon National Forest, near Lake Superior.

Water Witch

MARIE ZHUIKOV

W hen she was nine, she got lost in a mirror.
The water was running in the bathroom sink.
Just through washing her face, she had lowered the white towel she was using to dry it off, when she looked up from the bathroom sink into the glass. She truly looked at her face—not just her blue eyes and brown hair, her nose with the slight bump in the middle, and the breadcrumb freckles dotting the tops of her cheeks—but her whole face, long and square-jawed.

She rested the towel on the edge of the sink, barely aware of the rushing sound of the water, and peered into her eyes, past her irises—a word she learned from her third-grade teacher—and into the depths of her pupils. They were dark—blacker than black. It was like they didn't stop at the backs of her eyes, but dropped much farther into her body.

The more she looked, the more her face seemed a jumbled assembly of random parts, her features disjointed, meaningless. They could have belonged to anybody or anything. They were not her. What was *her* was inside her eyes.

Although she was a child, she was old enough to know about death. At church, the minister talked about going to heaven. Try as she might, she had never felt a heaven inside of her—no bright lights or rainbow walkways, only darkness, a stillness—the state of *not being*.

She knew someday both this inner "her" and outer "her" would not exist. Someday, they would be snuffed out—the depths inside her turned into a darker nothingness.

Nothing. Someday, she knew, she would be nothing. She blinked, scared by the feeling opening within her like a black hole.

From outside the bathroom came a soft "mew," followed by the thud of a furry body rubbing low on the closed door. The sounds brought the girl back to herself.

It was Muffin. The calico, green-eyed cat was her constant companion, especially since her brothers and sisters had grown and moved out. That left her—the baby of the family—alone with her parents. She didn't open the door to the cat, but she did turn off the faucet, and she kept staring into the mirror.

She didn't mind her mom and dad, but they didn't seem interested in her. Old and tired, they had started their family late in life. Now they had no motivation to do things with her, as if her brothers and sisters each packed some of her parents' energy in their suitcases and took it with them when they walked out the door.

She wondered what would happen when she left home. Would her parents shut down, or would energy flood them because their responsibilities were lightened? If they shut down, they would feel what she was feeling now—what it was like to be dead.

She wondered if other kids thought about death. If they did, they didn't talk about it. But she couldn't help it. Death demanded she think of it, and think of it *now*. Was it the dead bird she had found below the kitchen window yesterday? Its small brown head was twisted at an odd angle. She had picked it up with her hands wrapped in paper towels and buried in the back yard, away from Muffin, who she knew would eat it.

The pale yellow walls of the bathroom blurred as she stared into her eyes again, tears forming at their corners. Her heartbeat slowed. She stood entirely still.

Someday I am going to die. It was a fact as sure as life. But she had always taken life for granted. The feeling of being alive flowed within her and around her like the white sheets her mother hung up to dry on the line in the back yard with a cool Lake Superior breeze wafting up the hill. As she ducked through them, the worn cloth was soft against her fingers and arms.

She lost track of time in front of the mirror. Eventually, she closed her eyes and pulled herself away. She hung the towel on the rack to dry, and left the bathroom.

* * *

As she walked between the east and west banks of the University of Minnesota on a bridge above the brown and roiling waters of the Mississippi, she thought of the time she got lost in the mirror. She stopped and looked over the railing. White streaks of foam eddied in the dark water flowing below. The river was high with early spring runoff, carrying a sporadic load of logs and branches.

At eighteen and in college, she was thinking about death again. Although she was studying life—of all things, biology—she was failing. She was doing well enough in her biology class, but the accoutrements were doing her in: the calculus, the chemistry—everything she had to take to retain the privilege of studying life. Her introductory classes were huge—sometimes three hundred people crowded into a lecture hall. It was hard to adjust. She was used to classrooms of twenty-five in her high school. She felt swallowed, forgotten, alone in the mass of people.

She did better in the labs because they were smaller, except for her chemistry lab, which held a hundred students. She should have dropped chemistry, but she couldn't bring herself to do it. The class was required for her major. She'd dreamed of being a biologist for years. She wanted to go into medicine, wanted to help people who were sick. Watching her grandfather wither away from cancer and the barbaric treatments—the chemo, the radiation—she knew there must be a better way, and she was going to find it.

But she'd also stopped going to calculus. Her professor was deranged, she was sure—parading in front of the class with an open fly, wearing a suit coat covered with chalk dust. He mumbled, "Hold the phone!" whenever an idea struck him or a student had the naïve courage to ask a question. His frizzy hair stuck out like a clown's. She had a hard enough time understanding math, much less calculus taught by an eccentric.

She was attending college on a scholarship. She had to keep a B average or lose the money. How could she do that now? Her English class was going well, and that was about the only one she could say with confidence she'd get a B in. She was on a downward spiral—on her way to losing her scholarship and choice of career. She didn't know what to do. Her dreams of becoming a doctor or a cancer researcher were dissolving. She couldn't sleep, she couldn't eat.

It would be so easy just to lean over the railing of the Washington Avenue Bridge and fall into the beckoning water—move with it to another place, another state of being. Falling would solve all her problems. She wouldn't have to feel bad for skipping class, wouldn't have to go through the work of finding another course of study, wouldn't have to tell her parents about her failure. She could just tip over and give in. She could lean a bit more. . . .

Although she was still at the railing, she could hear the wind rushing through her ears—feel the terror of sudden weightlessness. She was falling, falling. Then came the hard smack of oblivion.

She stepped away from the railing and walked backwards, heedless of the passersby, until she hit the cold metal wall of the median walkway. As she stood staring out over the river, the feelings she had just experienced started to run in reverse: the oblivion, the weightlessness, the rush of wind. She breathed hard as overwhelming sadness enveloped her. As weightless as she had just been, now she felt heavy. So very heavy. Tears blurred her vision. Worthlessness worked on her insides with blunt, gnashing teeth.

She raised a gloved hand to her chest to slow her breathing. An older man dressed in a black wool coat eyed her quizzically as he passed. She waved him off, then put her hand back on her chest. She turned and began walking across the bridge, toward the side of the river that held her dorm. She stumbled a few times, still spooked.

What had *that* been? It was like she'd actually jumped. The experience had been so real. It had been almost like looking into the bathroom mirror and feeling what it was like to die. There was no way she was going to jump now. What she had just felt was too scary—too tangible.

When she arrived at her dorm, it was lunch time. She couldn't eat. She went to her room instead, lying on her bed and closing her eyes against the lingering sensation of falling.

Sitting in her own oasis of silence amid the chatter in the dorm cafeteria the next day, she read in the college newspaper that two days ago, a young man had jumped off the Washington Avenue Bridge . . . and died.

* * *

Five years later, she was staying in a hotel in Milwaukee on a two-week detail to the regional office of the Forest Service. She had graduated from college—enduring the humiliation of bad grades, changing her major to English, and almost losing her scholarship. Somehow, she had pulled herself together enough to find another path through her life and career.

She only needed to go back to the feelings she had on the bridge that day to spur her to keep going. She was thankful that what she felt then scared her so much she couldn't go through with her own plans.

She sat on the hotel bed, watching evening television, waiting for her bath to fill so she could shave her legs. For this regional office detail, she needed to trade in her field uniform for nylons and a dress. Although she was more comfortable in her handmade Red Wing boots and her institutional green pants and shirt, she welcomed the temporary change. It would be good to get a taste of how most of the workaday world lived.

The regional office was in what other Forest Service employees referred to as the "Milk of Magnesia" building —a structure built of glass, blue like its namesake. Some would say the contents within it provoked a similar laxative effect on the digestive systems of its inhabitants.

Her assignment was to prepare a briefing book about the Midwestern national forests for the Forest Service chief's visit next month. She was an agency public affairs officer, meaning she was basically a PR hack, but one that got into the woods fairly often. For three years, her home had been the Superior National Forest, along the shores of Lake Superior near Duluth, Minnesota. To complete her detail, she would need to bug the other eight PAOs for information and then edit what they sent into a cohesive whole for the chief. It was a job the regional office staff didn't have the time or inclination to do, and she was willing—eager to show her value.

She looked around her room at the faded red bedspread and the worn, dark red velvet curtains. She was in the heart of downtown Milwaukee at the historic Pfister Hotel, only four blocks away from Lake Michigan. When she had arrived, the Victorian lobby was crowded with convention-goers. From the elephants she saw on nametags and signs, she assumed it was a state Republican convention. The check-in clerks remarked how lucky she was to have a room because they were so full. Chandeliers hung over potted palms, dark oak desks with marble tops, and oriental rugs. A grand piano graced the mezzanine floor. Ornate murals lined the ceiling.

Overwhelmed by the ambiance and the crowd, she hadn't had a chance to notice what the murals depicted. But she saw that the paintings hung in gilded frames on the wall showed themes of bounty—a woman sitting at an overflowing dinner table, a man holding so many fish his arm bowed. They seemed a throwback to the wealth of natural resources long gone.

Her room was modest, with a tired elegance. She had to stay within the government rate, after all. It was only large enough for a double bed, a dresser, and a bathroom. The bathroom sported a claw-foot tub and a floor covered in old-fashioned white hexagonal tiles with black grout in between. Her window looked out on the tarnished copper dome of a cathedral and sooty skyscrapers. It was spring. The snow was gone, but the trees had not yet awakened. They stood in mute gray hope, their branches raised to the overcast sky like skeleton fingers.

She arose and checked the tub. It was full. She put her razor and can of shaving cream on the edge, pulled off her tennis shoes, then stripped off her jeans and sweater. She was tired after the seven-hour drive and hadn't eaten much. She slipped into the hot water. It took a chill out of her bones she hadn't known was there. A mist of steam escaped and floated toward the ceiling. Despite the warmth, as she studied the sterile white wall tiles and white shower curtain, she shivered.

She sank lower into the tub, gazing at the hot and cold water spigots and the spout. Reflected in the water, they looked like a gray face with a long nose that was looking at itself. She closed her eyes. After a few moments a heaviness overtook her—a slow sinking, like the very air was pushing her down, down, down—under the water. She tried to open her eyes, but it was as if the steam had glued them shut, licking her eyelids like the seal of an envelope. Her limbs were paralyzed, and she was sinking. As she struggled, an equal feeling of acceptance fought her efforts. Her heart pounded, although her body lay perfectly still in the water.

She felt gooseflesh break out on her arms and legs, but she couldn't open her eyes to see it. A voice inside her said, *This is how it ends. This is how it should be.* The voice wasn't male or female. It welled from inside her, yet seemed to come from elsewhere. She wanted to fight the sinking, but it pulled her deeper and deeper underwater. She could feel the waterline inching up her chest, then her shoulders, then her neck.

She didn't understand what was happening. She didn't want to die, not like on the bridge. Relentlessly, the slow sinking continued. Water inched up to her chin. Sorrow and self-loathing washed over her, like waves in the tub.

This is how it ends. This is how it should be.

She struggled to open her eyes, and once again, failed. Her heart beat faster as the warm water reached the sensitive skin of her lower lip. She had to get out. She had to awaken from this weird dream or whatever it was, or she would drown. If she had been able to move her arms, they would have been thrashing.

An image entered her mind: a naked woman in this very tub, long red hair splayed underwater around her head, her arms outspread on the tub rim, blood spurting from deep slashes in her wrists. Bright-red spatters festooned the stark white of the tub and tiles, spreading in the water. The loathing she had felt was replaced by peace. A deep peace that beckoned her—lured her to join it.

She tried to twist her body, get away from this vision. Instead, the water rose to cover her upper lip. It was just below her nose now. A little farther and she wouldn't be able to breathe.

What would happen then? She didn't want to find out. With all her might, she tried to sit up. But it was as if a rhino were sitting on her chest, gray, heavy and impersonal—like a thousand-pound afterthought.

Was this how it would end? Drowned in a bathtub under a phantom rhino? She didn't want to go that way. This was stupid. She struggled some more—tried to raise her eyelids against the heavy lethargy holding them down. It was no use. She couldn't move.

The water inched up her nose. She was able to tip her face up just the teeniest bit. She took a huge breath —one she hoped would last long enough . . . to what? To live. She wanted to live. More than anything else in this world, she wanted to kick the shit out of the water, get out of this tub, dry off, and *live*.

The bath water was over her nose now.

The whisper came again: *This is how it ends. This is how it should be.*

No it's not! she screamed in her head. *I want to live, dammit!*

Her anger broke through whatever was holding her down. As her nose and mouth surfaced, she took a huge, gasping breath. She scrambled to position her arms and legs under her. Her arms slipped, and she slid underwater. Flailing, she got them under her body and pushed herself up and out of the water. Legs beneath her, she carefully stood so as not to slip again. She climbed out of the tub, grabbed a towel, and ran out of the bathroom to her bed. Curled up into a shivering ball, she lay covered only with the towel.

Later, she calmed down enough to dress and to decide to request another room. When she went to the lobby it was empty—the convention-goers were attending some other function, no doubt. Voice low and serious, she grilled the clerk about whether anything unusual had happened recently in her room.

He couldn't meet her eyes when he told her a suicide had been cleaned up the night before—the shower curtain replaced, the tiles scrubbed. He explained they had to give her that room because the hotel was so crowded with the convention. After further grilling, the clerk told her the suicide had been a woman. With red hair.

Eventually, he looked into her eyes. Whatever he saw in them made him give her another room. A last-minute cancellation, he said.

* * *

Over a year later, she lay on a towel in the warm sand next to Lake Superior. Waves lapped gently and the sun beat down on her back. It felt so good after the long winter. She looked at her watch. It was two o'clock on a Saturday. Plenty of time remained to enjoy the day.

She turned her head and looked at the contours of her man friend's taut stomach as he lay on his back on a towel next to her. He caught her look. "Hey, my lady, what are you thinking?"

"I thought that was my line," she teased, lifting up on her elbows. "I was just thinking it doesn't get much better than this."

"Got that right." Galen ran his hand through his sweaty, dark hair and rested his arm behind his head.

They had started dating the previous summer after meeting at a mutual friend's party. They had been inseparable ever since. He was funny, smart, considerate, and damn good-looking. She couldn't believe her luck. He supported her in her job, even when she had to leave town to work as a public information officer on forest fires out West.

He was a sports reporter for the Duluth newspaper. Although their professions overlapped, he never had cause to cover any of her Forest Service stories, so they were cool where conflict of interest was concerned. But their jobs had enough differences to keep things interesting.

A trickle of sweat ran down her neck and collected in her tankini, between her breasts. "I'm going in the water to cool off," she said.

"Be my guest." Galen gestured toward the lake. "It'll take a while longer before I'm to that point."

She took off her watch, then got up and brushed the sand from her suit. Her hands lingered around her chest and hips—giving him a show just to torture him. He made a swipe as if to grab her and she jumped away, laughing. She turned and started toward the water, which was only a few yards away. The air was still, and she knew from her earlier toe-dip that the water was warm for once. She might be able to just walk in and dive versus her usual method of wading in slowly, stopping every few feet until her legs got used to the bone-chilling temperature.

She took a few more steps, and without warning, a wave of sound ripped through her, like the sonic boom of the jets she'd watched fly over her house as a child. The force of the sound knocked her down. She sat on the wet sand a moment, stunned.

An image of her friend Jacob flashed through her mind. He lay on a bed with a gun in his hand, his head a bright bloody mess mixed with gray chunks. Her stomach lurched.

She had met Jacob on her last fire. They had worked together in Colorado for ten days, staffing the information office—answering reporters' questions and calming residents' fears about a wildfire that was uncontained for days.

"Are you okay?" Galen put his hand on her shoulder and walked in front of her. He crouched to get a better look, concern clouding his eyes. She shook her head, leaned to the side, and emptied the contents of her stomach onto the sand.

Galen stood and stepped back, waiting to approach until after she was finished. "Baby, what's wrong?"

She clutched the sides of her head. She closed her eyes, hoping it would remove the vision of Jacob, dead on his bed. It didn't help. Jacob had been so happy-go-lucky. This just didn't make sense.

She gave a low moan. Galen's hands were warm on her shoulders. "Should I get help? Do you need help?" he asked.

She didn't know. What help was there for this? She shook her head, not wanting to draw more attention. She managed to open her eyes, gradually losing the image of Jacob as she took in Galen's concerned gaze. She moved her hands from her head to Galen's arms. Her tongue worked words through her sour mouth, "I think something just happened to one of my friends."

Galen arched his eyebrows in a question.

"Jacob," she said. "I met him during that last fire."

"Come on," Galen started to stand, giving her a tentative pull. "Do you think you can get up?"

She slowly stood, allowing him to help her. They walked back toward their towels and sat. Galen hugged her close. After a few moments, she said, "I saw him shoot himself . . . in my head, I saw him do it. The sound of the gun knocked me down."

Galen stared at her. "Shit," he said. "Do you have his number in your cell? You should try calling him."

She thought for a moment. All the information officers had shared each other's numbers during the fire. She hadn't deleted them yet. Jacob lived in Missouri—same time zone. Her purse lay on the end of her towel. She rummaged through it, found her phone and selected his number. But she knew even before she dialed there would be no answer. She folded her phone, looked at Galen, and shook her head.

When she called the number again the next day, a man answered with a muffled, "Hello?"

She introduced herself explained how she knew Jacob. The man said he was Jacob's father.

"Have you heard, then?" The father's voice was still distant, as though he were talking with the phone held a yard away from his mouth.

Her guts rumbled and turned over. "I'm not sure. Did something happen to him?"

"Jacob had . . . he'd been struggling with depression for several years," the man said. "He'd cover it up with jokes and laughter. But yesterday . . ." He took a deep breath. "Yesterday, he took his life. Now, we'll never hear his laughter again." His voice trailed off.

In the silence, her stomach flipped a second time. She pressed a hand to it and said, "You might find this weird, but I think I felt it." She couldn't bring herself to say, "when he killed himself," so instead, asked, "Could you tell me what time it happened?"

"They think it was just after two o'clock," his father said.

* * *

During the next few days, she tried to make sense out of these "episodes." First had been the bridge jumper, then the woman in the hotel, and now Jacob. With each one, the person's death was progressing closer in time to her, until Jacob's, which seemed to have happened in real time.

What was the point in her experiencing all these feelings and seeing the suicides, especially if she couldn't do anything about them? And why her? Why now? Her life was good. She had a job she liked, a man she loved, and she was living in a place she considered home. Why all this weirdness? It made her feel powerless.

She searched the Internet for meaning, typing in words like "feeling suicides" and "suicide clairvoyance." There was a lot of information on suicidal feelings, but that wasn't what she was looking for. News stories talked about people committing suicides after meeting with clairvoyants—perhaps the people learned something they'd rather not—but nothing about clairvoyants who felt actual suicides.

One story popped up that piqued her interest. It came from a local history page and described how, in the early 1900s, cities like Chicago and Duluth, which were at the tips of large bodies of water, were meccas for people with special abilities. Water was thought to magnify people's psychic abilities.

Something clicked in her head. *Water.* Each of her incidents had involved it: she'd been walking above the Mississippi River the first time, been near Lake Michigan and in a bathtub the second, and on the shore of Lake Superior for the third. Even when she got lost in the mirror, she'd been at the bathroom sink. *Water.* That had to be the catalyst.

So what to do? She couldn't avoid water for the rest of her life. Even on wildfire duty, plenty of water was dropped from helicopters and carried on the backs of firefighters.

Was she indeed a clairvoyant—a clear-seer? It certainly felt like it, although she didn't want to be one.

Galen was concerned yet understanding when she told him what Jacob's father had explained, and that she needed some time alone to figure things out. She didn't want to go "off" when she was with him and get him worried again. She needed more answers.

* * *

Walking along Lake Superior at Stoney Point just outside the city, she knew she was asking for trouble being near water. But she needed to think, and she couldn't do it indoors, especially on such a beautiful evening. Clouds glowed pink and purple from the setting sun, washing their color into the lake. Several small families played on the rocky shore. She hopped from boulder to boulder, passing the old fish house that stood in historical testament along the secluded harbor.

She chose a flat rock, still warm from the day's sun, and sat with her knees drawn up, looking to the lake. The sound of the lapping waves calmed her scattered thoughts. A few white gulls glided past on their way to wherever they spent the night. As the cloud colors started fading, the families gathered their children and left.

Soon, she was alone. Peace spread within her, almost making her feel like her problems didn't matter—like there were answers all around, if only she would look. The breeze whispered words in her ears, indistinct and distant.

After a while, she relaxed and closed her eyes. That's when she saw the man.

Tall and lean, he unfolded from a rusty red truck and made his way over the boulders to the beach, carrying a backpack. He sat on the stones facing the water like she was. After a few moments, he opened the pack and took something out. The dim light made it hard to see what he was holding, and his body blocked her view. Even though her eyes were still closed, she leaned forward as if to see better. It worked. Then she wished she hadn't. Her blood chilled and a burst of adrenaline rushed through her when she saw the gun.

Immediately, she opened her eyes and stood, looking over to where the man had been in her vision. No one was there. She was breathing hard now. She looked around to see if the man was somewhere else on the beach. No one. No red truck.

She stood for a few moments, not knowing what to do. She felt in her pocket for her cell phone . . . just in case. Her heartbeat started to slow, and she was about to sit again when she heard a vehicle engine and tires crunching on the gravel road. It was a red truck with rust patches.

The truck stopped and the tall, lean man got out. Without thinking, she unpocketed her phone and dialed 9-1-1.

"Nine-one-one, what is your emergency?" The female dispatcher's voice sounded distant and rather bored.

"There's a man here on Stoney Point who's trying to commit suicide. He has a gun!"

That woke the dispatcher up. "Stoney Point? Do you have an address?"

She looked around wildly as if to find numerals posted on the fish house or a tree. Of course there weren't any. "Ah, no. It's just off Scenic Drive 61 between Duluth and Two Harbors. Hurry. He's pointing the gun to his head!"

The man was still making his way through the rocks, but she knew he would pull out his gun soon. What should she do if he got the gun out before the responders could arrive? She hoped he was only intent on doing away with himself and no one else.

"I'm notifying the Two Harbors police," the woman said. "They should be there shortly. Ma'am? Ma'am?"

She realized the dispatcher expected a response, but her focus was on the man. "Yes?" she whispered into the phone.

"Stay on the line, please."

"Shouldn't I try and stop him or something?"

"No, ma'am. You'd better leave that to the police. You don't know what his state of mind is."

Ah, but she did. The familiar feelings were coming— the self-loathing, the hopelessness, and an immense weariness. The man was sitting by the water now, dropping his pack next to him. She knew there wasn't much time. She strained to hear approaching sirens, but only the gentle sounds of waves reached her ears. She started walking toward him. As she picked her way over the boulders, she saw him open his pack.

"Hey, nice evening, isn't it?" she called.

The man started and turned toward her. She was close enough to see the surprise on his face.

"Ma'am? Ma'am?" The 911 dispatcher's voice came faintly from her phone, which was now at her side. She quickly put it in her pocket.

The man didn't respond. But she knew she had to keep talking to him—had to keep him from carrying out his plan. She gestured to the sky, "Look, there's still some purple left from the sunset. Did you see it earlier?"

The man's voice was strained, as if it cost him a great deal to speak. "No, I didn't see it. Guess I was too busy driving." He brought his hand to his chin, which was grizzled with brown stubble.

She was almost to him now. "I love coming out here. It's so peaceful."

He gave her a look like he wished she would leave him in peace. *Sorry pal, no way*, she thought. "Mind if I join you?" She stopped a respectful distance away.

The man hesitated. "Really, I'd rather you didn't."

"Okay." She smiled and raised her hands, as if in surrender. ". . . Just being friendly."

In the distance, she could hear sirens—from more than one car. Relief flooded her. He didn't seem to hear them yet.

She needed more time. "I'll go back over to my spot." She nodded in the direction she had come. "I drive out here from Duluth sometimes. Where're you from?"

The man pressed his lips together, clearly not wanting to answer. Quickly, she said, "Oh, there I go, being nosy. Sorry. It's a bad habit."

Something softened in the man's gaze. "No, it's all right," he said. "I'm just visiting, from St. Paul. I come up here to get away. Guess I'm not feeling sociable right now."

"No problem." She turned and started walking back to her rock. Once she got far enough away, she removed her phone from her pocket and put it to her ear.

"Ma'am?" the dispatcher repeated.

"Yes, I'm back. I hear sirens, they're coming."

"You didn't talk to him, did you?"

"Yes, but it's okay. I bought us some time."

She glanced back at the man. He was still sitting with his pack closed. Now he looked toward the road, seeming to hear the sirens.

"Are the squad cars there yet?" the woman asked.

"Yes, they just pulled up. I think everything's going to be okay." By now, she had arrived back at her rock. She sat down.

"You can sign off now, but stay in the vicinity in case the police want to talk to you."

"You got it," she said, and closed her phone. Then she saw the man open his pack, take out his gun and point it at his head. Her heart clenched and went cold.

Her first impulse was to run and take the gun away from him, but that was too dangerous. She prayed the officers would reach him in time. It seemed to take forever for the three of them to get out of their cars and notice the man on the beach.

One officer, who was tall and built like a Mack truck, started jogging toward the man who was facing away, looking out over the water. The other two fanned out and approached slowly from the sides.

The tall officer, gun drawn, stopped a few yards away from the man. She could hear him say, "Sir, this is the police. Put down your weapon."

When the man made no move to comply, the officer said, "Sir, I'm not sure what's wrong, but this is no way to solve things." His fellow officers were closer now, guns drawn, too.

A wave of nausea worked on her stomach. She didn't want to see the aftermath of this scene, like she had with Jacob—his brain splattered across his bedroom wall.

The man's back and shoulders shook, and he drew in a great breath. Then he yelled, "What's the use?! What's the use of any of it?" He turned his face, misshapen from his outburst, to the officer, but kept his gun to his head.

Then, seeing the officer had a gun pointed at him, the man hesitated and seemed to deflate. He lowered his gun limply to his lap, turned to face the lake, and slumped.

The officer moved in slowly, talking so low to the man, she couldn't hear. Whatever he said, it seemed to work, and the man placed the gun a few feet away on the rocky beach for the officer to grab. By this time, the others had moved in. They kept their guns trained on the man until the tall officer had the discarded gun in his grasp.

She let out a deep breath and lay down on the rock, looking up into the darkening sky that held the promise of stars. She hoped now the man would get the help he needed.

A certainty settled within her that the progression of the suicide timeline would stop. This was as far as it could go—allowing her to see the event just before it happened.

The voice that was neither male nor female seemed to come out of the breeze and speak inside her head: *There will be others like this man.*

With these words, part of her became weary. Another part—energized. She had her home, her career, and she had Galen. Now, it seemed, she had her purpose.

There will be others like this man. . . .

This is how it should be.

END

Marie Zhuikov is a novelist, poet and science writer from Duluth, Minnesota. Her poems have appeared in several anthologies and community projects. She's written two eco-mystic romance novels set on Lake Superior and published by North Star Press: *Eye of the Wolf* (2011) and *Plover Landing* (2014). *Plover Landing* was nominated for a Northeastern Minnesota Book Award. Zhuikov has a BA in science journalism and an MA in public health journalism. She currently works as a science communicator for the University of Wisconsin Sea Grant Program in Superior, Wisconsin. This is her first short story. Visit marieZwrites.com to learn more.

What a Fire Weighs

JOHNNA SUIHKONEN

Many months ago, my friend Ishkode told me of a place where all lost things could be found. "It is here," he said, "enshrouded in the spirit waters of Lake Superior, where you can mend your spirit." Somewhere, inside of me, I had tucked away this advice, like a note from a close friend.

I moved to Northern Minnesota a few months ago hoping to escape the chaos that can be found in bustling city life. I had hoped to find myself among the silence of the woods. To find myself at peace among the bark of the ancient forest, the primordial bedrock, and the pristine waters in the heart of the Northwoods. I was in search of clarity.

Long overdue for a northern wayfaring, I packed the necessities among rain gear, snacks for the road, and a new book containing the geology and history of Lake Superior into my evergreen-colored daypack. I clipped my Nalgene to my pack and slung my Nikon over my shoulder with finality.

I threw my pack into the passenger's side seat and crawled in. Inserting my key in the ignition, the car stirred, then started. Folk music hummed from my speakers and my car was filled with the warmth of wonderment and adventure. Driving down Highway 61, tamaracks, pines, and poplars provided a sense of comfort as I watched hues of green streak my window like rain on a spring morning.

When I arrived at the trailhead, birch trees rested alongside the path, heaving with each gust of wind. The trees stood stoic; gurus with grave faces. Between the leaves, the sun glinted through, causing momentary blindness and warmth to settle over me. Berry bushes, picked clean, straddled the edges of the path. I made my way through the wooded land with quiet, confident steps. I heard the wings of a black-capped chickadee among the backdrop of silence.

After a short time, I reached the trail that would cut down to the lake. It was an entanglement of protruding rock formations and sheets of slate, heavy with the scent of pine. I made forward movement down the arduous path by stepping sideways, cautiously sliding one foot and then the other.

When I reached the bottom of the trail, the trees opened up, giving way to the sacred lake. It stretched on for miles, throwing back the image of the serene, open sky. On the horizon, the lavender sky and cerulean sea blended, like watercolor paint pooling on canvas; an orchestra of color. Sleepy waves kissed the dappled shoreline. I had never seen a body so boundless. So sweeping. The vastness enveloped me, leaving me wordless at the remarkable beauty of nature. Wind. Water. Earth. Fire.

Removing my shoes, I exposed my bare feet to the grace of the Earth. When I dipped my toes into the water, it was colder than I expected. Ice. At this thought, I felt a sudden surge; a life force undulating through my body. *I'm alive.* Standing amid my own reflection, a numbed face stared back at me from the cerulean water. In the depths of the water, something had caught my eye. Swiftly, I reached down to grab the small stone from the water and then placed the stone in my open palm. Entranced, I admired the intricate bands of white amid brilliant oranges and reds. A striking similarity to fire.

I tore open my pack wildly, tearing through my bag, searching for the guidebook I had packed this morning. I flipped through the book until I found exactly what I had been looking for. Running my index finger down the page, I reached an image of the stone that looked most similar to the one I held in my palm. Comparing its resemblance to the one in the guidebook, I read:

> Lake Superior Agate: created from gas bubbles that formed more than one billion years ago, when the North American continent began to split in two. These gas bubbles, or vesicles, became filled with iron, quartz and other minerals . . . 10,000 to 15,000 years ago, glaciers sailed south and carried these agates along with them.

At the words "split in two," I felt the weight of absence. The concussion started in my heart and moved outward until I stood frozen, unable to move. A flashback to the moment I said, "You need to leave" and the long-winded chain of events that followed. A series of short experiments to replace whatever it was I had lost. Between each short experiment, I experienced the crippling thought that what I had lost was him. Time and time again, I'd try to find my way back. I became overwhelmed by thought. All at once I felt the ache of absence. It's miraculous how the absence of something can feel so heavy. One of the universe's numinous mysteries, I suppose.

Growing up, my father had always told me not to play with fire. "Fire," he said, "has the potential to destroy." Fire always fascinated me—the way it could be felt, even from a distance. The way it could be manipulated; nurtured, and extinguished.

All those years that I played with fire, I was the one in control, I thought. For years, I watched the fire burn. Stuck within its wrath, I watched, suspended in time. Pieces charred and writhed and floated away, like ashes on their final flight.

In the beginning the fire was warm, comfortable, and even soothing. As months passed, the fire quickly grew, becoming uncomfortable—even controlling—and all-consuming at times. I continued to seek the gentle fire I had once known. Nurturing fires became a skill of mine. Not just his, but others', too. What happens when you try to keep too many fires burning at once? One of two things: a wildfire or you run out of kindling. Neither of these were desirable outcomes.

I think back to the moments that were much like drowning. Another numinous mystery. How is it that you can be drowning and not even recognize this until your head is above water again? Until you've cut the anchor from the rope that tied your ankles together and held you submerged beneath the water's surface? Resting safely on shore, underneath the light of the sun, you remember the weight of the darkness that lives in the space beneath the water's current.

I examined the small stone I held in the palm of my hand, closely inspecting the bands compiled of years and composed of various minerals. It became apparent that I had vesicles within me, too. Over time, these vesicles had become filled with the leftover pieces of people, places, things, and ideas other than my own. Some of these pieces were admirable. Others were less so.

What I never realized, until I stood there with that small stone, was that the weight of absence did not belong to him. Along the way, I had lost myself. It was pieces of me that had charred and writhed and floated away, like ashes on their final flight.

Reawakening to reality and all the beauty that surrounded me on this day, I tucked the stone in my pocket.

Maybe, much like the small stone that was now resting in my pocket, a human is a conglomerate of all the experiences their heavy heart holds. A human is the person they want to be, but also the person they didn't want to become. Under the weight of the world, we are prone to become less admirable version of ourselves. Sometimes, we don't even recognize these versions of ourselves. In the same thought, it became clear that, without pressure, many of the natural things that exist in our world would not be the very thing we admire. I became drenched in this thought.

As the sun settled into the horizon, the rocks glistened, reflecting the citrine sky. I cupped my hands together and scooped up a small amount of water. Bringing my hands to my face, the water trickled down my cheeks, gently kissing my chin. My eyelashes were sodden to the touch.

As I sit here now with my eyes steady on the stippled shore of Lake Superior, I realize that what I've lost can be found again. The loss no longer bears the weight of a burden. Instead, it carries the power of a gift.

END

Johnna Suihkonen says "What a Fire Weighs" is an interpretation—literal and metaphorical—of her experiences in the Northwoods of Minnesota. She has spent the last eight years living in Duluth and Ely, Minnesota. During this time, Lake Superior has been a continuous source of inspiration and the place where her soul resides. She is currently a middle school English Language Arts teacher in Ely. When she's not teaching, she enjoys camping, hiking, photography, drawing, and writing (in many forms).

On My Head

THERESA ALLISON-PRICE

I don't know how long I have been standing here, my feet in the water, a cold spray from the waves on my face, the sun warming the top of my head. This is just where I have always been.

When the skies are clear I can see Canal Park and watch the lift bridge make its slow climb to let ships through. In the winter the lake freezes and large slabs of ice stick up like teeth biting the sky.

People come by sometimes. A young man used to come and sit on my head, stretching his bare feet out to feel the warmth I absorbed on a hot day. Sometimes couples would come strolling along the shore and climb up one side of me, jumping down on the other side to find a nice little place hidden from view, where they could cuddle and kiss.

Still, I was lonely. There are no other large rocks like me nearby. I stand alone with the pebbled shore on either side of me. I have heard the people talking as they walk by me, saying there are places up the shore where there are lots of large rocks and a lot more people, and I've wondered what that would be like, to not be alone.

I am out of the way, hidden. You have to climb down a steep bank or walk a ways along the shore from another access to find me. I was pondering this one day. The winds were strong and the waves high, splashing against me like a wall of ice, so high that sometimes the icy fingers would even reach the top of my head. There were no people around this day; the waves were too big for them to stumble across me along the shoreline. The lake was being so mean to me, hitting me in the face like that, and I was already so sad. I wanted to cry.

That was when she arrived. A girl who couldn't have been more than thirteen. She was short and plump, her hair a shaggy mess. She came climbing down the steep bank through the trees from the park above, slipping the last foot in the dirt and falling on my head. She looked around, pulled her knees up into her chest and started to cry. I cried with her.

A few hours later the wind slowed, the waves began to die down, and the girl's sobs subsided. She wiped her face with her sleeve and patted me on the head.

"Thank you," she said. She rose to her feet and started climbing back up the muddy bank, using the small trees to help pull her along. I felt a warmth inside my cold, stony self. I had helped her. I hoped she would return.

The days slipped by, but I didn't forget about that girl. Rocks have long memories, you see. Every day I waited, hoping. The short, warm summer began to grow colder, and still I waited. Then finally one day she was there again. She came down the steep bank, more carefully this time. She found a nice spot on my head, toward the front where I jutted out over the lake, and she sat.

She sat for hours, writing in a notebook, pausing occasionally to look out over the water and pull her jacket tighter around herself. Then she set the notebook aside and stretched out her legs, dangling her feet over the edge of my head in front of my face.

"There's something magical about this place," she said, smiling. I smiled, too.

She visited regularly after that. In summer she would turn up almost every day, but even in the subzero winter months she would never stay away for more than a few weeks. In winter she would stand on my head throwing snowballs out onto the lake, trying to break the ice. During the warmer months she would linger longer, writing, napping, and sometimes crying. I didn't know for certain why she cried, but I thought she might be lonely, too. She was always alone when she came here.

I watched as she grew into a woman. She stayed short, but her extra padding turned into curves, and she learned to manage her shaggy hair. Occasionally she would bring a guitar and strum it clumsily while she tapped her foot on my head. The sounds were mellow and slow.

Then one day she didn't come alone.

"It's just down here." I heard her voice as she half climbed, half slid down the steep bank, using trees to steady herself and slow her descent, swinging, like a monkey. She came out on the top of my head like always, and then reached to help a young man as he stumbled clumsily down to join her. They laughed when he nearly tripped and she stopped him from falling. He brushed his hands on his pants and walked to the front of my head, looking out over the water.

"It's really beautiful," he said.

She smiled and walked up next to him. "I've never brought anyone here before."

"Well, I'm honored," he said, smiling at her.

She found her favorite spot and sat, cross-legged. He sat next to her, and they talked for hours.

After that day the girl started visiting less often, but she would still turn up every few weeks or so, sometimes alone, sometimes with the young man. One day the young man showed up without the girl. It was a warm summer afternoon. He spread a blanket out on my head and took sandwiches, fruit, and cheeses out of a basket. A few minutes later the girl emerged from the trees.

"What's all this?" she said.

"Lunch." He took her hand and seated her on the blanket, nestling down next to her, one arm around her waist. They ate, talked, and laughed. When they finished he helped her to her feet and then knelt in front of her.

"Marry me?" he asked.

"Of course!" she blurted. He stood to kiss her. I was happy for my sad little plump girl. She would never feel lonely again, and now I had two friends to visit me!

It wasn't long after that the girl quit visiting me altogether. Every day I waited, hoping she'd turn up with her notebook or guitar to keep me company for a few hours. The days turned to weeks, the weeks to months, and the months into years. Years that went on and on, and still my friend did not return. With each passing season I grew sadder, and the loneliness I had once known so well settled back into the cold stone of myself. I quit noticing the moods of the lake and the warmth of the sun on my head.

A few people came by. A college-age boy sat on my head for a few hours one time, and I thought he might come back, but he never did. It was just as well, I didn't like the smell of his cigarettes, or the way he put them out by rubbing them on me, leaving a black mark for the rain to wash away. Groups of tourists would come by once in a while and take pictures of the lake, but when they saw me blocking the shoreline, they always turned around and went back the way they'd come. No one visited me like that plump little girl had.

One day I heard the trees rustling and voices coming down the bank.

"Careful," she said. I recognized her voice, older now, but still the same. The young man came out of the trees first, but he wasn't as young as he had once been. He had less hair on his head and more on his face, with specks of gray mixed in. He reached up into the trees and helped another plump little girl, about thirteen, find her footing safely from the bank onto my head. She looked just like the girl I had once known. Behind the girl came a little boy, a few years younger, giggling as he slid a bit in the mud. His mother's hand caught his arm from behind, keeping him from falling, and then she emerged from the trees as well. She looked older, too, a little heavier, a few wrinkles near her eyes but still as beautiful as she had been the last time I had seen her. She smiled as she stepped into the sun.

"I used to come here all the time when I was your age. After your grandma died," she said. Her daughter ran to the front of my head and plopped down, reaching her toes out past my face, trying to touch the waves. "Your dad even proposed to me here."

The man put his arm around her and kissed her forehead.

"I've missed this place," she sighed.

"When we move here from Boston this summer can we come here all the time?" the little boy asked.

"Sure, kiddo," my old friend said, messing up her son's hair.

"Cool," he said and sat next to his sister.

"Maybe moving here won't be so bad." The plump little girl giggled as a wave licked her toe. "There's something magical about this place."

She smiled.

I smiled, too.

END

Theresa Allison-Price grew up in a small town near Eau Claire, Wisconsin, and has spent most of her adult life in the Duluth area. She has a degree in anthropology from the University of Minnesota–Duluth and is a certified veterinary technician, but what she always wanted to do is write fiction. At twenty-nine years old, this is her first published piece, and she hopes there will be many more.

The Lake Effect

MAXWELL REAGAN

1919

The *S.S. Murdock* was somewhere off the coast of Grand Marais along the southern shore of Lake Superior when the snow began to fall. The steamship had found itself in the middle of an unpredictable storm that had risen within the last hour. Heavy waves plowed against the ship, churned by the intense wind that sped upwards of sixty miles per hour. Due to the quickly dropping temperature, mist from the waves formed into ice that fell in clusters upon the deck. The thermometer had plunged twenty degrees in the last eight nautical miles.

Being towed close behind the *Murdock* was their companion, the *S.S. Moss*, a schooner stripped of its masts to transform it into a barge capable of carrying large cargoes of lumber. The *Moss* was considerably slowing down the progress of the *Murdock*, making it extremely difficult to combat the raging storm. The heavy surf was battering both ships, but the *Murdock* was really struggling from the tremendous load it was towing. The fifteen-man crew aboard the *Murdock* fought to stay on top of the storm, all doing their part to keep the ship afloat. The ship's captain was confident the veteran steamship, which had a lengthy career as a lumber hooker on the Great Lakes over the past three decades without incident, would make it to the safe haven of Whitefish Bay.

The captain of the *Murdock* was James Tucker, a former naval officer in his youth turned shipping captain, navigating the open waters of Lake Superior for the past two decades. He was a single man without a family. He was a rather rugged-looking middle-aged man with a gnarly, unkempt beard. The man wore a navy blue hat atop a thick crop of long, greasy brown hair. Under the man's left eye sat a rather large scar that gave him the appearance of a fearsome Ahab. Captain Tucker's conduct, however, was that of a gentleman. His courageous, paternal demeanor put him in favor of the crew, some of whom looked up to him as a father.

"Nothing to be concerned about," the captain told the helmsman with confidence. "We've been through much worse. Just keep the ship steady. We don't have enough time to turn around. We must bear onward."

"Captain, I don't know how much more the ship can take. We're rocking like a cradle here. One big wave might roll us," warned the helmsman, his face painted with trepidation.

"Nonsense!" cried the captain. "If we plow through the waves, that should help stabilize the ship. Please, take charge. I will be right back."

Captain Tucker exited the pilothouse in desperate need of speaking with the chief officer. Heavy snow fell in every direction from the gray skies above. Even though the sun was not visible at the bleak and gloomy horizon, they were fortunate to have what little light was left.

The wind whipped the water and ice with such force it stung the captain's cheeks. Snow and ice stuck to his beard like paint, giving him, perhaps, a more distinguished appearance. The wind whizzing by coalesced with the crashing of the waves to create one incessant soundtrack of chaotic noise. The Witch of November reared her ugly head, blowing about the surface waters and spinning up thirty-foot waves. Each time the ship's bow plowed its way through a wave, water would splash up over the ship and rain down as cold slush and ice. The captain boarded the stairs down to the deck, trying not to slip.

Crewmembers shuffled about the deck, some using shovels to push the snow and ice back into the lake while others frantically tried to secure the lumber and other cargo on the deck. Heading toward the back of the ship, the captain opened the door to the crew's quarters, pushing his way past the galley and down into the engine room. The chief officer was directing the engineer to keep a close eye on the boiler.

The engine room, the foulest place aboard the ship, was filled with the stench of human sweat and bunker fuel. The roaring of machinery made it almost impossible to hear one's own voice. Metal moved and rubbed. Pistons turned and churned up and down vigorously, like a steaming locomotive. The hissing scream of hot steam erupted from the boiler. Pipes, valves, and gauges; levers, buttons, and knobs complicated the engine room. Not a single man on board could completely read or handle the machinery alone.

"How are we holding up down here?" yelled the captain. "Any problems?"

Startled by the captain's appearance, the officer, a larger man with hands stained black with oil and grease, jumped. He wore glasses so completely fogged with condensation that the captain could not see his eyes. Taking off his glasses, he nervously cleaned the lenses on his filthy coat.

"I apologize for the scare, chief. I just wanted to make sure everything's running smoothly," the captain said, not sure the man had heard him.

"No, Captain, I apologize. I'm full of unease. Nothing major yet, but the boilers are having a hard time staying hot with the dropping temperature. Our engine's working on overload. And the crew's concerns are worsening by the minute. I don't know what to tell them, sir."

"All right, listen," said the captain. "We don't have much farther to go to get to Whitefish. We just need to make it there, and we'll settle 'til the storm passes. It won't be much longer. Just tell them to hold tight and stick together, and we can make it. You understand?" he yelled over the noise behind them.

"Captain—"

In that instant, the ship was struck by a wave that nearly knocked the captain and the officer off balance. The officer looked scared, but the captain stayed courageous.

"Tell them to hang tight," shouted the captain. "I have to return to the helm."

He darted back to the deck with a fierce stride. Walking across the deck past the cargo, he couldn't help but look into the face of each crew member he passed. Fear-stricken faces, pale in the fading illumination of the setting November sun. Looks of terror and desperation, like children in the midst of a nightmare. Foundering was a strong possibility on everyone's mind, even Captain Tucker's, but he knew now wasn't the time to lose hope. They only had twenty-three miles to go.

Before reentering the pilothouse, Captain Tucker paused. The sun was setting, even though he could not see it. Snow blew in every direction, creating a strange filter, like the view from inside a snow globe. The lake churned and seethed, throwing and tossing waves that smashed against the side of the ship. The wind that rolled in from Canada blew snow and ice about like confetti. Clouds passed overhead with steady ease. It was almost a moment of benevolence. The captain was able to find the beauty among the chaos, and he reveled in it, just for a moment.

Superior had a sublime effect on the captain. Never before had he taken the time to look in admiration at the natural wonder of the great lake. However, his admiration for Superior was quickly overshadowed by his fear of her capacity. He knew how unpredictable and heedless she could be. To him, Superior was an ocean as big as the Atlantic. Even though he had been a captain for twenty-three years, he still had a hard time stomaching all that water.

The captain refused to succumb to nervousness. Perhaps it was his respect for Mother Nature, but he was well aware of the dangers before them. The captain had heard the stories of ships and crews taken captive by the lake. Up 'til then, there had been over thirty documented shipwrecks in Lake Superior. Everyone on board remembered the White Hurricane, which just a mere six years before ravaged the Great Lakes, taking 250 lives and foundering twelve vessels, two of which sank to the bottom of Lake Superior never to be seen again, or the *Mataafa* Storm of 1905 that claimed thirty-six lives and ran six ships aground.

What the captain found unnerving was that most who lost their lives to the lake were seldom seen again. That was the strange effect of Lake Superior; it had a tendency to keep its victims. With an average temperature of forty degrees, the water temperature kept bacteria from growing and forming the gas that allowed bodies to float to the surface. Because of this, some believed bodies swallowed by the lake might actually remain preserved, intact, floating just below the surface. They lurked in the murky depths of Lake Superior like ghosts frozen in time, sitting undisturbed, just waiting to be recovered.

Captain Tucker feared that if his ship were to capsize, this would be his fate. Like a true captain, he would go down with his ship, and Lake Superior would take him under, allowing him to sink to his own watery grave. He foresaw those who would talk about the lost ship captain who sank in Lake Superior. The idea that the lake that gave him purpose and livelihood could come full circle and be the source of his demise was defeating, but his fear did not stop him from fulfilling his purpose of traversing the rocking waves and strong currents of the Great Lakes.

"You got everything under control?" asked the captain, entering the pilothouse.

"Hardly. The upwind and waves are tossing us about like a ragdoll," replied the helmsman.

The helmsman, a young man, stood, knees quivering. The only thing holding him up on his rubber legs was the helm he braced himself against. His blond hair fell in front of his eyes.

"Just keep it up. You're doing a fine job. Only a little farther to go."

The captain, anxious and jittery, pulled a bag of chewing tobacco out of his back pocket. He took out a wad of moist snuff and secured it under his lip. He sighed in a moment of ease and relaxation. However, the moment was short lived.

"Uh . . . captain?"

"I see it."

Not far in the distance a towering wave was approaching. Closely, they watched as the wave came barreling toward them, knowing there was nothing they could do. In agony they waited as the wave grew bigger—a thirty-five-foot wall of water aimed at the port side of the ship. For the captain, time seemed to slow down. He had minutes to think his way out of this situation, but his mind was frozen.

The wave crashed into the boat, and the captain gutted his tobacco into his stomach. The wave hit with such force it crushed one of the lifeboats, washing debris and water onto the deck. The captain and the helmsman stood blinking, surprised they were still aboard and that the boat was still afloat.

"I knew she could handle it!" cried the captain.

He looked behind them to see that the *Moss* was still afloat, too, trailing behind them. For a moment, Captain

Tucker thought the worst might be over. He was confident the *Murdock* could take whatever Lake Superior had to throw at her.

After about ten more miles, the helmsman felt the port side dip toward the water, throwing off the *Murdock*'s center of gravity. The old steamship began to slow considerably, down to about three knots.

"Captain, she's pulling to the port side, and she's losing speed!" screamed the helmsman.

"What the hell is going on down there?" cried the captain. Using the voice pipe, he called down to the engine room, "Everything okay down there?"

It took a moment before he heard a faint voice from the other end. "It's not looking good. The seams are leaking along the hull here and freezing along the port side. Our pumps can't keep up. The engine's slowing down because of all the ice."

"Shit," muttered the captain under his breath. "Keep her going as long as you can and keep me posted. Since we're taking on water, we should shut the valve on the pipe here and communicate via messenger. I'm going to radio the *Moss*. Keep me posted." The captain closed the valve on the voice pipe.

"Jensen! Radio the *Moss*!"

The radio operator had been so quiet he was all but invisible to the other two men in the cabin. He stood silently watching out the windows, rubbing his hands over his hairless scalp. The gaze of his dark-brown eyes was fastened upon the incoming waves, always disappointed to find another wave waiting for them just behind the next

one. The operator stopped looking at the raging water
and sat down at the radiotelegraphy.

"What message do you want to send?" asked Jensen.

"That we're taking on water and need to drop them
off at Vermillion Point if we want any chance of making it
to Whitefish."

The radio operator carefully crafted the message
using Morse code. Dots and dashes beeped. The captain
watched as the light flashed on and off, speaking an eso-
teric language he would never fully understand.

It wasn't long before the *Moss* messaged back. The
light bulb flickered on and off again as the beeps came
in. Just as quickly as the message came in, the beeping
ceased.

"They are ready, Captain," said the operator.

"All right, give them my instructions."

The captain gave the orders as the radio operator
furiously put in the correct amount of dots and dashes to
articulate the message. It was complete, and the plan was
set in motion. The plan was to bring the *Moss* closer to
shore so she could anchor and turn her bow toward the
waves and ride out the storm while the *Murdock* made a
mad dash for Whitefish. They were going to be cutting it
close, but the courage of Captain Tucker gave a sense of
optimism to the operator and the helmsman.

"Time to bring her in. Let's drop her off within the
next two miles," the captain said to the helmsman.

They brought the *Moss* inland and detached the haw-
ser, allowing her to be cut loose. The *Moss* let go, and slowly
the two ships departed from each other. They lingered only

a moment before the old steamship left in a fight to get to Whitefish Bay. The *Murdock* continued eastward as fast as her engines could. Waves continued to rock the ship in a rapid display of rage. The captain, the operator, and the helmsman all turned behind them to watch the *Moss* drop her anchor and turn her bow into the waves, lifting up the ship only to fall back down with a crash. The daylight had all but disappeared. The bleak atmosphere painted the grim scene of misery and woe. They all remained quiet and gave their thoughts and prayers to the *Moss*.

The room was silent except for the roar of the wind against the pilothouse windows. As darkness engulfed them and the snowflakes became larger, their vision fell to next to nothing. The captain felt blind. He looked out the windows into blackness and stood face-to-face with the unknown. Nothing was certain, even his own beliefs. It made him lose faith. Nobody said anything, sharing the feeling that nothing anybody could say would change the mood in the room. The captain, the helmsman, and the operator all stared into blackness, nearly catatonic.

In the snowy distance, a larger passing ship spotted the struggling *Murdock* along the shores approaching Whitefish Point, just a stone's throw from Whitefish Bay. The *Ara*, a broad steamship in freshly painted metal, was seeing its first season on the great lake, shipping over 50,000 tons of iron ore from Duluth. Inside the *Ara*'s helm was calm. The strong steel held the ship steady against every breaking wave. It wasn't until that the ship got closer to the *Murdock* that the pilot noticed the old steamship was progressing at an unusually low speed.

"Captain Louis, there appears to be a ship in need of assistance on the starboard side." The pilot motioned for the captain to come look.

"Ah, yes," said Captain Louis slowly, squinting in the glass. "It appears so."

"Should we help her, sir?" asked the pilot.

"I suppose it's our duty to," he expressed drily.

"What should we do, Captain?" asked the concerned pilot.

"Pull up alongside her and shield her from the incoming waves. That's all we can do at this point."

The *Ara*'s captain stood back, folded his arms and watched with disinterest as the rescue effort began.

Maneuvering the *Ara* through the turbulent waves, the large steel ship approached, slowing her engines to match the pace of the splashing *Murdock*, pulling alongside. The *Ara* shadowed the *Murdock*, providing temporary shelter from the tumbling waves.

Captain Tucker was relieved by the *Ara*'s approach. *Perhaps five more miles, maybe less*, he thought. *We'll make it.* The waves were being broken up by the *Ara*'s large hull. The *Murdock* was now much steadier, but still in trouble. The bow of the ship had become so heavy with ice and water that the old *Murdock* was beginning to nosedive into Superior.

"Come on, old girl! Hang in there!" yelled the captain, slapping the control panel in front of him.

Just as the words left his mouth, the oiler walked into the pilothouse. The man's trousers were soaked and stiff from the knees down. He removed his hat when he entered and clenched it between his hands.

"Captain," the oiler said, "I come bearing bad news. We've been taking on a lot of water. The water has almost reached the boiler room. I give us less than twenty minutes before the boilers extinguish or explode. I'm sorry."

A long silence passed. The captain said, "Get the crew together. Get the lifeboats ready."

The oiler left in a hurry. With only miles to go, Captain Tucker still believed they could make it. But he knew the crew was scared. He wanted to give them the best chance. He wasn't worried, figuring that the *Ara* would pick them up as soon as the lifeboats were launched.

Captain Tucker left the pilothouse, going out into the storm. He watched the crew scramble across the deck in all directions.

Even though he looked the part of an adventurer, Captain Tucker knew his life had been rather mundane. The only waters he knew were the waters of Huron, Erie, Ontario, Michigan, and Superior; nothing as deadly as the seven seas. He felt like a sleepwalker, just running through the motions of life, with nothing for him to hold onto other than his job and the lake—the only two things that gave his life purpose. He was disappointed that neither had ever given him anything in return.

However, now, with the possibility of death within reach, he had never felt more alive, more awake. Superior had given Captain Tucker a different purpose: to survive, and to survive long enough to save his crew.

One lifeboat had already been deployed. The last lifeboat was being loaded when the chief officer yelled up to the captain, "WE ARE ALL READY DOWN HERE!"

The captain went back into the pilothouse.

"All right, boys," he said, addressing the operator and te helmsman, "they're ready to abandon ship. Time to go to the lifeboat."

The two men left their posts and bolted toward the door. The helmsman hesitated before exiting the door, and the two men looked behind them at their captain standing resolute in the middle of the empty room.

"Aren't you coming, Captain?" asked the helmsman.

"I think you already know the answer to that, son," the captain replied.

"Captain! There's more than enough room in the boat," exclaimed the operator.

"You don't get it, do you, boys? This is my purpose. I'm responsible for the ship and everyone on board. It's my duty to hold out to the bitter end and see this thing through. Or I will die trying. Now hurry! Or they'll leave without you."

They both bid the captain farewell, and he thanked them for their faithful service. The two barreled down onto the deck. The captain watched the last two men climb into the lifeboat. As they slowly began to lower themselves into the bucking waves, he yelled over the chaos, "SEE YOU ON THE MAINLAND, BOYS!" as the crew struggled with the lifeboat's tackle and went into the pilothouse one last time.

The *Ara* left behind the *Murdock* in an effort to retrieve the two lifeboats, one departed and the other making its way to the lake. With the *Ara* gone, she ceased to offer the *Murdock* any more protection. The ship came to a crawl before it slowed to a speed of next to nothing. Only the waves propelled the ship. Slower and slower she went until she began to heave drunkenly in the water.

Even though the *Murdock* had almost made it, she was no match for the lake. The captain stood at the helm looking out into the blackness of the storm. He thought about how cold the water must be. He thought about drowning. He thought about sinking to the bottom.

The final wave came without warning. It took the ship up to where she hung for just a brief moment before slipping into a deadly trough. The crash was just too much for the aged wood. The top of the hull shattered like glass, gushing in water. The lifeboat still not detached from the ship pounded against the side.

It did not take long for the rising water to reach the pilothouse. The ice-cold water flooded around the captain's ankles. But he wasn't thinking about himself; all his thought were for his crew. Would they make it? If they didn't, he felt his sacrifice was for nothing. At that moment, the captain did not feel fear, only regret. So many choices in his life he wished he could take back. So many decisions he didn't make he wished he would have. Everything seemed so clear in that moment that he wished he could have lived every day like this, with death at his shoulder.

Meanwhile, the crew in the lifeboat desperately tried to cut the ropes attached to the ship, but it was thick and half frozen. The turbulent surf made it next to impossible to keep a steady hand. The first lifeboat wasn't far away from the ship, its occupants watching the sinking vessel in horror. Lumber and wreckage washed into the lake, surrounding the wreck in a debris field that was quickly becoming an obstacle course.

The final moments happened quickly. The stern of the *Murdock* rose up sharply, and the pilothouse almost completely submerged. The *Ara* tried to offer assistance to those in the first lifeboat by throwing ropes to the soaked sailors. The men's hands were so frozen they could not grip the tightly wound hemp.

Then the rushing water finally reached the boilers. The deathly cold lake water hit the scalding boilers, causing them to erupt in a powerful explosion. The pilothouse in which Captain Tucker stood blew apart, sending the captain and large pieces of the ship one hundred feet up and out into Lake Superior.

From that point, nothing kept the ship from sinking to the cold silt bottom of Whitefish Bay. The *Murdock* joined the ghosts of several other vessels that had sunk in the Whitefish area in the past half century.

The whole ordeal was over in a mere five minutes. Miraculously, the second lifeboat had managed to detach itself from the sinking ship just in time, but found itself stuck in water littered with wood and debris.

Captain Tucker was immersed in water so cold it was like an electric shock to his nervous system. His chest constricted and tightened. He had the sensation he was being bound by strong ropes. What came next was pure instinct. He couldn't help it. His lungs were in a desperate need of air, so he opened his mouth, taking in a large gulp of ice-cold lake water. Kicking and flailing, he hopelessly tried to surface for air, but kept hitting a large piece of the ship. He knew what was about to come next: a freezing cold death followed by a deep plunge to the bottom of this immense body of water, where he would remain for the rest of time.

Even though he knew what was about to happen, Captain Tucker didn't truly know what was awaiting him at the bottom of that lake. What was after that? That he was in the dark truly scared him. *What's the point?* he thought. *Death is inescapable, why fight it?* He couldn't help but reflect on his wasted life. However, he felt something deep inside him: an urge and will to live. It was all he wanted.

The captain swam and scoured the waters for an opening to the surface, until he felt his hand brush a piece of rope. In a vain and desperate attempt for air he gripped the rope and pulled himself to the other end, hoping it was attached to a floating piece of the ship. With blackness blotting his mind, he surfaced, gasping for air and coughing up water.

Climbing onto the top of a floating roof section of the pilothouse, he found relief from his immediate discomfort. He kissed the lumber in thanks for making it out with his life. He took a moment just to lie atop of the roof and let himself be washed in the waves, gasping when they hit him.

A few minutes later, Captain Tucker raised his head to see the *Ara* floating nearby, perhaps fifty yards ahead, her crew watching the lifeboats battle the wreckage and remains. The rescue ship did not attempt to offer assistance, or perhaps they could not. Tucker could scarcely see the two lifeboats surrounded by long timbers of Norway pine and large chunks of wood paneling. His crew frantically waved at the *Ara*.

Captain Tucker drifted closer to the large steel ship and looked up from his patch of floating roof to see two heads pop over the side of the ship.

"Hold on," yelled one of the men.

"THROW ME A ROPE!" shouted Tucker over the roar of the storm.

The two men looked down at Captain Tucker.

"PLEASE! JUST TOSS ME A ROPE!" again screamed Captain Tucker.

The other man looked down and yelled to Tucker. "I will have a boat sent for you."

The two men's heads disappeared back over the railing, and the steamship pulled away from the wreckage. Captain Tucker was left adrift, alone among the angry waves and freezing November snow. He crawled to the middle of his makeshift raft and curled into a fetal position to stay warm. His hair had already frozen. He knew it wouldn't be long before he would become a solid block of ice.

Ashamed he'd let down his crew, he feared they were goners like he was. "Cowards," said the captain out loud, shaking his fist at the *Ara*. Captain Tucker could not imagine how the *Ara* could leave his crew stranded in the water or why the crewmen did not toss him a rope. It seemed as if fate was working against him. All he could do was think about the suffering his crew was enduring because of his decision to beat onward instead of turning around.

Time passed, and the boat the *Ara* promised to send was nowhere to be found. The storm had died down to a light snowfall, and the waves ceased to offer any more harm. The captain kept drifting atop of the pilothouse roof, lost in the currents and his thoughts, which revolved around three things: where his crew was, how cold he was, and how long it would be before he died. How long he had been floating on this piece of roof, he did not know. It felt as if it could have been hours, but he wouldn't have been surprised if it was just a matter of minutes.

The captain floated in and out of consciousness, not fully aware of what was real and what was not. Lying adrift in the darkness listening to the wind and waves and feeling the snowflakes upon his face, he felt a strange calm. Warmth spread throughout his body. It was pleasurable, but the captain knew that feeling warm was one of the final stages of hypothermia.

The captain's mind focused on one blinking light that appeared off in the distance. Half conscious, half dead, the captain stared at the small beam of light, considering that it might just be an illusion. His first instinct was that it was his mind playing tricks. Not until about the tenth time the light blinked did the captain realize it was a lighthouse. It must have been the Ille Parisienne lighthouse in Whitefish Bay.

He slowly watched the light grow larger and knew he drifted closer. The light shone down like a twinkling star in the night sky, a beacon that seemed to draw the captain in. Even though the captain was near death, he still had a glimmer of hope to hold onto.

Finally, the light became so bright it engulfed his entire vision. Light beams radiated in all directions, a blinding brilliance righteous as the morning sun. It warmed the captain inside and out. He could feel the lake pulling him into the water. He didn't fight it.

Then he felt a pair of hands on his back. Something picked him up. He felt weightless. It was unlike anything he had ever felt before. The hands gently set the captain down again as if in a dream. When the hand slapped his frozen cheek, though, he awoke from his daze.

"Can you talk to me?" said a voice. "Holy shit, Tom, his clothes are frozen to his skin."

The captain opened his eyes slowly, blinded by light. He could make out a man with a mustache, wearing a thick pair of glasses and kneeling over him. "Jesus H. Christ . . . you're alive?" the man said.

"D-D-Did . . . they ma-make itah?"

"We haven't found your crew yet, but they can't be far. We need to get you to a hospital. You must have someone up above looking out for you," said the man. "You're sure lucky. Most could not survive a night in those waters."

The small yawl left the Ille Parisienne lighthouse and headed toward Sault Ste. Marie with Captain Tucker alive and wrapped in blankets in the back. He looked over the rear of the boat, back on the journey he had taken. He scanned the horizon in search for his crew's lifeboats. Nothing. The morning was strangely quiet. The sun slowly rose in an array of orange, pink, and gold. Tucker eyed the Ille's dense evergreens and rocky coast. He finally got a look at the lighthouse that jutted into the bay. It was painted red and white, like the *Murdock*. Small waves hit the shore before finally breaking into a wash of white and blue. The captain wondered how something so beautiful could cause so much destruction.

The crew of the *Murdock* was never found. The lifeboats were simply gone, not even an article of clothing left behind. It is believed by many, even Captain Tucker, that his crew succumbed to the deadly lake effect of heavy snow and massive waves. Legend has it the crew lies just a mere sixty feet under the surface of Whitefish Bay, among a graveyard of other victims—still surrounding the wreckage of the *Murdock*, preserved in the deadly cold waters of Superior, hoping that one day their captain will return.

END

Maxwell Reagan spent his first eighteen years in the suburbs of St. Paul, Minnesota. After graduating high school in 2013, Max attended college at the University of Minnesota–Duluth. Now going into his senior year, he hopes to graduate in the spring of 2017 with a Bachelor of English degree with minors in journalism and film studies. One day he would like to pursue a career in professional writing. This is his first publication.

The Heart Under the Lake

ERIC CHANDLER

Childhood is like a mild case of stupidity. Kids don't have any experience. They can't put things into context. For example, when Doug lifted the top of his desk and discovered his lunch was gone, he just sat there. He stared dumbly at the front cover of his spiral notebook on top of the pile. No brown paper bag. He looked up confused.

Farther up the row, as the other kids lifted the pale wooden tops to their desks, he saw Brittany with the platinum blonde ponytail grab her lunch bag. He watched as she pulled the tab off a can of orange soda. He'd had an orange soda in his lunch.

"Mrs. Lundquist?" He raised his hand.

"Yes, Doug?"

"My lunch is gone."

The teacher came down the aisle from her desk at the head of the room. She lifted the top of Doug's desk and looked at the front cover of the same notebook. They both looked around the desk and under it. It was a mystery. Doug was disappointed an adult didn't have the answer. They always had the answers.

They closed the desk, and Mrs. Lundquist walked back to the front of the room.

All the other kids looked silently at Doug. Then they turned back to their peanut butter and jelly like hyenas. He looked up and noticed Brittany was finishing a sandwich with cold cuts. Like his mom usually made for him.

Then she pulled a miracle from the bag: a whoopie pie. A big white layer of frosting encased in two big slabs of chocolate. Like an oversized Oreo.

He slowly realized Brittany had taken his food.

On the playground after lunch, he confronted her.

"You stole my lunch."

"No, I didn't." She shoved him with both hands in the chest.

A pack of girls formed behind Brittany. Why was the new kid hassling Brittany?

"I suppose your mom gave you an orange soda."

"Yes. An orange pop."

"And a ham sandwich."

"Yup." She crossed her arms and smirked. Half of the pack did the same.

He was stumbling, but he had the kicker in his back pocket.

"Your mom gave you a whoopie pie, too?"

"A what?"

"A whoopie pie. It's like a big chocolate sandwich."

"Yes. My mom gave me one of those, too."

The pack turned and left Doug standing there. He was positive she stole his lunch. Too many coincidences. But, like most rookies facing the Big Lie for the first time, he wasn't sure anymore. Even though they were unique to Maine, Doug guessed Minnesota had whoopie pies, too.

He shrugged his shoulders and headed for the teeter-totter, still hungry.

* * *

You've seen a standing wave. You probably just didn't realize it. If you move your coffee cup back and forth at just the right frequency, the brown caffeine climbs up one side of the cup and then the other. The level in the middle of the cup stays exactly the same. There's a formula for the time period of that wave. It depends on the length of the enclosed body of water, its depth, and the acceleration of gravity. This phenomenon is called a seiche (pronounced "saysh"). A Swiss hydrologist coined the term in 1890. It means "to sway back and forth." The hydrologist studied lakes in the Alps that showed this behavior. There's another word you know that'll help you remember the meaning and how to say it: slosh.

* * *

Sometimes, after school at John A. Johnson Elementary, Doug walked downhill with his buddies to the Dairy Queen. It took less time for him to walk home than it took to ride the bus. They had time to hang out and still got home at the same time. He always bought a Mr. Misty. His mom never figured it out.

After they bought their treats, they went to the far corner of the parking lot. A retaining wall dropped past a steel railing. They slurped through their straws, finished their drinks and cones, and talked about whatever kids talk about in third grade.

When it was time to beat the bus home, Doug threw his cup and straw over the edge into the pile of garbage at the bottom of the wall. Weeds and grass, brush and trash. Cigarette butts and Mr. Misty cups.

They split up and spread out through the small grid of streets called Two Harbors. Doug walked up the hill to the high school. In a few months, they would sled down that hill. He walked around the rectangular building and down a few blocks to his house.

It was small home but clean, thanks to his mom. It was the same little white house in every new town they lived in. Doug's dad couldn't hold a job. He was always employed, but his work came as a series of jobs in rapid succession all over the map. It was hard on Doug and his younger sister, Karen. Every year or two, they had to break into a new social circle.

Doug walked from the alley past the detached garage and into his back yard.

"Hey, Doug."

"Hi, Mr. Nelson." Doug ran into the neighbor's yard and threw his books onto the picnic table.

Earl Nelson worked strange hours. He was a fireman on the crew of the *Edna G.* She was the steam tug that helped maneuver ore boats into the docks. Some said she was the last working coal-fired tugboat in all of the Great Lakes.

Earl asked, "I ever tell you how I lost ten pounds in five hours shoveling coal into the *Edna G?*"

Doug smiled and said, "Yeah, yeah. A million times. Big rescue." Earl put coal to her that time like other people's lives depended on it. Because they did. There was a ship adrift without power and headed for the rocks. They saved her.

That was the first story he told to Doug like an adult. Now, Earl brought it up once in a while so Doug could feel like he was in on a joke. Earl thought Doug could use a little training on how grown men banter since Doug's dad was never around. But Earl had no idea what it was like to be the new kid. He was born and raised in Two Harbors.

They sat across from each other at Earl's picnic table in the warm, early September sun. The green grass and leaves looked tired, like they'd had enough. Not changing color, but close.

Doug looked at the fork and empty paper plate in front of Earl. "What was that?"

"Blueberry pie."

"Was it good?"

"Yes, sir. Mrs. Nelson makes great pies."

Three or four flies buzzed around the plate.

"Want to see a trick?"

Doug said, "Sure."

Earl pulled a small jackknife out of his pocket. He unfolded one of the blades and held the knife in his giant hands. Earl claimed he could tear a quarter in half. Fingernails blackened with coal dust. Skin callused and cracked from stoking that furnace in the belly of the *Edna G.* Of course he could tear a quarter in half. Doug didn't even think of asking him to prove it.

He held the knife in his right hand between thumb and index finger like he was pointing to one of the flies. It looked like a toothpick in his huge mitt. He inched his hand along the top of the picnic table. The fly faced away from Earl's hand and the knife. It wiped its head with its forelegs.

Earl pressed the knife down in slow motion and cut the fly in half.

Doug's mouth hung open. "It didn't even try to get away."

"They can see everywhere except right behind."

The screen door squeaked open at Doug's house.

"Doug. Come do your homework." Houses so close together, his mom didn't have to raise her voice.

"Okay, Mom." Doug picked up his books.

Doug's mom smiled and waved. "Earl."

"Janice," said Earl, as he waved back.

"Bye, Mr. Nelson," said Doug.

"Don't work too hard."

Doug laughed. "I won't."

After supper, Doug's dad herded everyone out to the garage. Doug and Karen jumped into the "way back," the back compartment of the Oldsmobile Delta 88 station wagon with the seat that faced backward. They drove down to the Dairy Queen and got soft-serve ice cream cones. Doug looked at the same woman who sold him a Mr. Misty earlier. She raised her eyebrows. Doug stared back, willing her to be silent. She didn't betray him. Nice lady.

They drove down to Agate Bay, the western of the two bays in Two Harbors. Doug's dad, Jake, parked the wagon across from the ore docks. Half a dozen other cars were already there. A laker was berthed along the dock closest to shore. A train full of taconite sat on top of the dock. One of the chutes folded down above the boat. There was a whoosh as the pellets roared down into the hold, leaving a puff of red dust floating behind.

Doug licked his cone and looked around the lot. Folks sat on the hoods of their cars, others behind the wheel. Some on the front bumper. All looking at the boat. Their faces were blank, like they were staring at a drive-in movie or a campfire.

Doug thought it was pretty cool. The last place they lived, they bought ice cream cones, too. They used to be the only family watching logging trucks dump pulpwood into a giant pile by a paper mill. Judging by this crowd, taconite was at least five times more entertaining.

As gravity pulled the ore into the belly of the vessel, Doug saw the *Edna G* sitting quietly at her slip, a thin, intermittent puff of smoke coming from the stack. Mr. Nelson had been down there earlier stoking the fire while the captain helped the laker into place. Some of the newer lakers had bow thrusters and didn't need a tug to help them. The tugboat sat there with the mustard-yellow trim around her wheelhouse and deep-maroon hull in the water. The same deep, rusty-red on the tug and the ore dock and the train cars and the hull of the laker and the taconite pellets.

The *Edna G* sat like a girl along the wall at a dance, waiting for a turn on the floor.

Doug looked at his dad. Jake stared at the tugboat.

* * *

The Devils Hole is an aquifer-fed puddle in a limestone cave east of Death Valley National Park. An earthquake in Mexico caused a seiche in that tiny pool that went back and forth for fifteen minutes. It shook up all the algae and sediment. Around a hundred tiny Devils Hole pupfish live in that body of water. If you were the rarest fish in the world that day, you probably thought the world was ending.

The 2011 Tohoku earthquake and the resulting tsunami off the coast of Japan killed over 15,000 people. The main island of Japan slid several feet laterally, and the earth shifted in its orbit. Across the globe, in a fjord in Norway, the water level along the shore went six feet up and down during the earthquake. Norway is 5,000 miles from Japan.

There's a zigzag lake on the south island of New Zealand called Lake Wakatipu. A seiche in the lake has a natural harmonic that's twenty-seven minutes long. The water rises and falls eight inches. Depending on the slope of the beach, that means the shoreline can advance and retreat ten or twelve feet. The hydrologists trot out all kinds of math and data in a 1955 paper on the subject. In the harbor in Duluth, Minnesota, the average amplitude of a Lake Superior seiche is between one and six inches. The natural period of this standing wave is 7.9 hours. Much longer than twenty-seven minutes.

The Maori people have a different explanation for the sloshing of Lake Wakatipu. They believe it ebbs and flows in time with the beating of a giant's heart at the bottom of the lake.

The Sibley Peninsula outside of Thunder Bay is thirty-two miles long. That's almost the same length as that whole lake in New Zealand. The stone profile of the Sibley Peninsula looks like a man lying down. It's called the Sleeping Giant.

The enormous heart of Lake Superior's giant must beat very slowly.

* * *

Doug sat up in bed. He wasn't sure why.

There was a scream from downstairs. His mom.

A deeper yell.

A breaking glass.

Doug ran down the stairs but stopped on the landing where the steps pivoted toward the front door. Jake stormed by and grabbed the doorknob. He didn't see Doug in the shadows.

He jabbed a finger back toward the kitchen and yelled, "It's always my fault. That's bullshit, Janice." He walked out onto the front porch and slammed the door behind him. The door didn't latch and bounced back open.

Janice walked to the door and onto the porch. Jake walked toward Burlington Bay, the eastern of the two harbors. Doug walked out and put his arm around his mom's waist, surprising her.

"Go back inside, Doug. It's okay."

Doug looked up at his mom's tear-stained face and then out at the spitting November rain. The wind howled from behind the house toward the lake. The porch was eerily calm in the lee.

Jake heard the wind whistle through the power lines. He walked through the trees to the rocky shore. White-caps rolled in the big lake as the gusts blasted him. He loved storms. They made him feel small. It was dark and almost freezing. Somehow, Jake found it all comforting.

The next day, the headline in the *Duluth News-Tribune* said: ORE CARRIER LOST IN LAKE SUPERIOR.

* * *

On November 10, 1975, those northwest winds had a 300-mile fetch down the whole length of the greatest lake. The wind and low atmospheric pressure caused the water to "set-up" on the east end. The seiche caused the water to rise three feet in Sault Ste. Marie, topping the gates of the Soo Locks and flooding Portage Avenue with a foot of water.

Theories abound about why the *S.S. Edmund Fitzgerald* sank. One is called the shoaling theory. Shallows called the Six Fathom Shoals northwest of Caribou Island lie near the path of the doomed laker. Because of the storm-induced seiche, the theory is the boat got damaged running aground there because the water was shallower than normal. The damage led to the shipwreck. Divers said the shoals didn't look like they were hit by anything. The shipwreck doesn't show damage that indicates she ran aground.

One thing is sure. Seiche or not, shallows or not, the water conspired with the wind and killed all twenty-nine of those men.

In 1844, the wind came out of the northeast, and the water stacked up in the southwest end of Lake Erie. Then, the wind abruptly changed direction and came from the southwest. The pent-up water launched like someone pulled back on a slingshot and let go. A twenty-two-foot seiche raced back to the northeast. It topped a fourteen-foot sea wall and plowed through the streets of Buffalo, New York. The water killed seventy-eight people.

In 1929, 45,000 people celebrated the Fourth of July along the waterfront in Grand Haven, Michigan. An early morning storm over Lake Michigan saw a seiche build twenty-foot waves that raged down the pier and the beach. The water killed ten people.

The wind and the waves don't care if you're on a ship or on land. They don't care about physics and resonant frequencies. They don't care what name you give them.

* * *

It was the Bicentennial. The *Edna G* was going to race against a pair of government tugboats. Jake was practically vibrating he was so excited. Doug, Karen, and Janice walked behind him as he led the way to the breakwater.

The breakwater in Two Harbors is like a big concrete left arm. It juts out from the east end of the harbor toward the lake and bends at the elbow back toward the west. It encircles most of Agate Bay and protects the ore docks and ships. There's a small lighthouse at the end. The concrete slopes down on both sides toward the water, and has a path along the top. On each side, there's a much narrower level area wide enough for one person to walk along just above the water level. Giant boulders along the base of the cement help disperse the energy of the waves.

Jake and his family walked past the boat launch and onto the breakwater. It seemed like the whole town was standing there to see the race. They squeezed their way out past the elbow. It was standing room only at the high point of the concrete. They looked to the east.

They saw a giant plume of black smoke first. Then, around the point from Burlington Bay, the *Edna G* came full steam ahead. Jake started shouting. Doug tried to picture Mr. Nelson shoveling coal into the fire as the tug plowed through the waves.

Doug moved closer to his mom. Janice held onto Karen. Partly because of the crowd. But mostly because Jake was screaming like a lunatic.

"Look at her go!"

Everybody in the family was smiling. From embarrassment. Jake was jumping up and down. Thankfully, the whole breakwater was roaring. The pride of Two Harbors was showing what she could do with a coal-fired steam engine. Jake actually blended in.

Doug wasn't sure where the finish line was, but the *Edna G* was so far in front that it didn't matter. The red-and-gold tugboat built in the nineteenth century won.

Jake pounded Doug on the back over and over again and shouted, "Wasn't that something? What do you think of that?"

Doug thought it was great, but his back stung a little. He wasn't used to getting slapped around like a grown man.

Everybody basked in the afterglow of the victory when there was a tremendous clap they felt in their feet. A giant wall of blue-gray water exploded into the vertical along the whole forearm of the breakwater. The wake of the three tugboats slammed into the whole length of the outer structure at once. People screamed. Several were washed into the lake. Even though it was the Fourth of July, the unlucky victims whooped from the shock of the frigid water. Jake ran down to the lower edge of the breakwater and climbed down onto some boulders. Janice held onto Doug and Karen and said, "Be careful" to Jake, but not loud enough to be heard. Jake reached out to a woman floundering in the water. He and some other men helped her back up.

All up and down the breakwater, clusters of people reeled in all the swimmers.

As they walked back to the house, Jake kept repeating, "She showed them." Janice was just glad they were away from the water and the kids were safe.

* * *

The U.S. Coast Guard cutter *Naugatuck* (WYT-92) lost to the *Edna G* in that race. *Naugatuck* means "fork in the river." She was built in 1939 in Bay City, Michigan. She had two diesel engines instead of steam and generated 1,000 horsepower. She had the typical USCG livery: Black hull with a red, white, and blue band. White superstructure.

Eight months before the tugboat race, *USS Naugatuck* was out of service in Sault Ste. Marie, Ontario, due to maintenance on her engines and rebuilding the bunks where the crew slept. Within minutes after the *Fitz* disappeared from radar, the crew scrambled to start a rescue. Late that night, they cranked her up. And immediately lost oil pressure on the right engine. After working all night, they got her fixed and headed out onto the now-calm surface of Lake Superior. They spent the next three days covering a search grid through the oil slick of the missing ship. They dutifully pulled debris from the water and brought it back to shore. The *Naugatuck* went out of commission in 1979, two years before the *Edna G* retired.

The U.S. Army Corps of Engineers tug *Marquette* also lost to the *Edna G* in that race. She was built in 1942 in Louisiana. Powered by a 960-horsepower diesel instead of steam. She had a black hull and a tan superstructure with red trim. In September following that race, the Minnesota Pollution Control Agency wrote a memo that said the *Marquette* was involved in dumping barrels of military waste into Lake Superior near the Knife River. The tugboat logs are missing now. Big mysterious controversy.

The *Marquette* retired in 1982 and was donated to the Lake Michigan Naval and Maritime Historical Society in Chicago. You can see her propeller at the Soo Locks. Someone reported her downbound past Detroit in 1996 on her way to some buyer in Key West, Florida. In 1997, her name was changed to *Mona Larue*. Some time after 2003, a tug named *Captain Diane* found the *Mona Larue* out of commission in Great Inagua in the Bahamas. They towed her to Haiti. Who knows where the *Mona Larue* is now?

Waves aren't the only things that bounce around.

* * *

Another little town. Another great lake. Another little harbor.

Janice found a job through a friend. It was at a place called Big Paw Resort on Lake Huron. She cleaned rooms and did whatever else they needed. Fetched groceries for the kitchen. She even learned how to drive a truck with a plow to move the snow.

The resort was a series of cabins right along the pale beaches just north of Harrisville, Michigan. They got room and board as part of the deal. Doug and Karen and Janice barely fit into the tiny employee cabin. They took their meals in the resort kitchen of the main lodge. There was no carousing.

Once Doug got boisterous, and the owners scolded him. The guests out in the restaurant didn't want to hear a screaming kid from behind the swinging doors to the kitchen. Doug and Karen looked at each other across the table and chewed in silence. Janice was glad all the meals were quiet. And grateful they had meals at all after Jake left.

Not long after they moved to town, Doug walked with Janice and Karen down to the harbor. A breakwater surrounded it. Dozens of men stood on the breakwater that fall while Doug's little family had a picnic. Wonderbread peanut butter and jelly sandwiches on a rare day off for Janice. They watched as the anglers cast some kind of heavy lure with multiple treble hooks on it out into the water. They stood still until the lead weight dropped to the bottom and the line went slack. Then the men reeled in some line and made violent backward motions with their pole, dragging the big hooks along the bottom. They hoped to snag a spawning salmon. Dozens of men, jerking back and reeling forward over and over. Once in a while they lifted a fish sideways or tail first out of the water.

Doug was getting better at carving out a niche in each new town. He saw *Star Wars* in the little theater with his new buddies. He bought a Case jackknife at the hardware store for $4.75 and tried to cut flies in half.

He rode his banana seat bicycle to the gas station. The attendant gave Doug and his friends old patched-up inner tubes from giant truck tires. They inflated them and took them down to the little town beach. They floated out into the grayish-green waters of Lake Huron. It seemed like a big stagnant pond. Chalky with gypsum. Or Doug was just spoiled after the gin-clear waters of Lake Superior.

One day, after they shoved their tubes into the woods, Doug and his buddies rode to an ice cream shop. It was overcast, but very muggy and hot. The shop was along the main highway that cut through town from Alpena in the north to Wurtsmith Air Force Base in the south. It wasn't a Dairy Queen. It was a locally owned geodesic dome. Doug was a classmate with the child of the owners. That kid wasn't there with Doug, but in a town of 500 people, everybody knew everybody. Even the new kid. Especially the new kid.

Doug ordered the clone of a Mr. Misty. His friends finished their ice cream cones in no time. Doug wasn't done yet. Brain freezes slowed him down. The guys saddled up on their bikes. It was time to go.

Doug looked around for a place to pitch his half-full cup. Back in Two Harbors, in the corner of the parking lot, everywhere was a garbage can. He saw a cylindrical container under a corner of the awning. The kind with a hemisphere on top with a side-facing, spring-loaded door that you pushed in to drop the garbage into the barrel.

He threw the cup at the can. It bounced off the lid and exploded on the cement. Red juice and paper cup and straw and ice in a giant splatter.

"Hey!" A shout from inside the dome behind the screen where you ordered your treats.

Doug stiffened. The other guys rode off. He wasn't near his bike.

His classmate's mother came out with bright red curly hair that matched the color of the roofing on the shop.

"What'd you do that for?" She frowned at Doug.

Doug was frozen in place.

She bent down and started wiping the pavement with a rag and throwing away the garbage. The place was neat and clean. Doug saw that now. It wasn't an open-air dump like behind the old Dairy Queen retaining wall.

"You got nothing to say?"

Doug stared back.

She shook her head. "What the hell's wrong with you?"

Doug ran to his bike and pedaled away. By the time he got to the cabin, his mom was already on the phone with somebody. He came in through the screen door, gently closing it so it wouldn't slam. Karen was in the corner with a doll.

Janice kept saying she was sorry into the phone. She stood next to a small table with her work clothes on. She hung up and looked at the wall. Suddenly, she sensed Doug and looked at him.

She put both hands up, covered her eyes, and started to sob.

Doug bolted out the door. The screen door slammed behind him. He ran until he stood at the shoreline. He looked out to where the gray-green water met the gray-black sky in a horizontal line. His teacher said that was the vanishing point.

* * *

Jacob Greatsinger was the president of the Duluth, Missabe and Iron Range Railway Company. They needed a bigger tugboat to replace the *Ella G. Stone.* She did well since 1884, but she wasn't tough enough anymore for the growing traffic fetching the iron ore. In 1896, they paid the Cleveland Ship Building Company $50,000 to build a new tug. One hundred feet long. People that saw her steam upriver past Detroit called her a "corker" and a "great combination of strength and elegance." They painted her the same maroon and yellow as the railroad company colors. Jacob christened the new tugboat in Duluth to honor his daughter, Edna.

She helped lakers in and out of Agate Bay. During a storm in 1905, the *Madeira* smashed up on the North Shore. The *Edenborn* ran right into the mouth of the Split Rock River. The *Edna G* rescued men from both ships.

That November storm killed thirty-six people. It led directly to the construction of the Split Rock Lighthouse that looks right down on the wreck of the *Madeira* today.

In November 1917, she steamed to Norfolk, Virginia. For two years she hauled coal barges up and down the Atlantic coast. Before she returned to Two Harbors in 1919, someone stole the big eagle off the wheelhouse. When she got home, it took two months to repair all the salt-water damage and fix her up. Then she went back to work. They never replaced the eagle.

The *Edna G* fought in the Great War and came home for good. Other than that two-year stretch, she spent her whole life in the Great Lakes. On Lake Superior. In Two Harbors. She's floating in Agate Bay right now. She still wears the colors of the Duluth, Missabe, and Iron Range railroad.

Missabe is what the Ojibwe called the low-slung hills of the Iron Range. Supposedly, it means "sleeping giant."

* * *

Doug parked his little Toyota in the same parking lot where he used to eat ice cream. He looked at Gina and tilted his head toward his door. She gave him the side eye and shook her head.

"Maybe sometime when it's not forty degrees and raining," she said.

"You'll miss all the fun."

She went back to her book as he opened the door and got out. He zipped his jacket up to his neck and put up his collar. He walked down the path toward the *Edna G*. She waited at her slip with that raised pug nose. That long, maroon swoop of her hull back to the stern. That mustard yellow. Her wheelhouse faced toward the lake. She surveyed the harbor she'd crisscrossed for a century. Her fire was out, but she looked ready to go.

He turned and headed to the breakwater. He thought about his mom back in Maine, the land of the whoopie pie, running that inn with her cousins. He thought about his sister studying to be a nurse. That day of the tugboat race was one of the last times he ever saw his dad.

He walked out to the elbow of the breakwater. He looked at the point where the *Edna G* roared into sight in the lead. Ten knots of wind blew directly into his face. Spitting mist. Overcast. The lake was a dark, gunmetal gray.

He squatted down and squinted into the wind. He was a hydrologist now. He and Gina were headed to Ely so he could work for the U.S. Forest Service. He wasn't sure how this California girl would handle northern Minnesota. He wanted her to stick around.

Doug watched the waves come in. The line of approach was perpendicular to the breakwater. He was a college boy. He knew physics. He knew what waves did when they hit hard linear surfaces. They came in, instantly reversed, and headed right back out. He watched a peak come in, rise up, and reflect. The waves were fine, unharmed. The waves bounced off with the exact same frequency, wavelength, and speed. The only thing that changed was their direction.

Even if there was no wind, Doug knew the heart under the lake would still beat. You might see the water pulse if you waited a third of a day. At the end of a three hundred-mile journey, the waterline might shift an inch. A seiche is both massive and, usually, almost invisible. You'd have to be patient and attentive to notice. If it was perfectly calm, and you were too, you might have a chance.

END

Eric "Shmo" Chandler is a husband and father who cross-country skis as fast as he can in Duluth, Minnesota. His work has appeared in *Sleet Magazine*, *The Talking Stick*, *O-Dark-Thirty*, *Aqueous Magazine*, *Great Lakes Review*, *Grey Sparrow Journal*, and *Northern Wilds*, to name a few. Visit ericchandler.word-press.com to read his published fiction, nonfiction, books, and poetry.

The Light

James Brakken

I knew well the back trail from La Pointe to my home. I had walked by many times over many years, often after dark without a lantern on moonless nights such as tonight. And, on those many walks, I had never before seen the glow of a light through the trees this far north of the small Madeline Island community. Thus, on that chilly April evening, when my eye caught the faint, warm flicker of what appeared to be an oil lamp in the woods, I was taken aback. So much so, it caused me to pause on the trail and peer as best I could between the bare oaks and scattered pines of the dark forest. Squint as I might, though, I could not discern the source of the faint glimmer. Unable to contain my curiosity, I stepped off the trail toward the distant gleam.

Confident I could readily return to that trail, I chose my steps with care, silently stalking the often-uneven glow. Each footfall brought me a bit closer to the source of the light—and a bit farther from the trail behind.

I soon realized my quest was more difficult than I had imagined. In the black of night, rocks and fallen tree limbs tripped and tangled my feet while low-hanging branches pulled at my coat and overalls. I soon lost my hat when a balsam bough swished it from my head, depositing it, I supposed, somewhere on the dark forest floor. I knelt on one knee and felt to no avail for the knit wool watch cap before resuming my pursuit of the far away gleam.

A hundred paces from the trail, the light became somewhat brighter. I clearly saw the flicker of an oil lamp now, its gleam coming from behind a windowpane. A cabin? A cabin out here? I stood in my tracks, bewildered, wondering how it could be I had never before seen or heard any sign of a dwelling in these woods. Certainly, on at least one of my many daily walks to the La Pointe fish cannery where I had worked for over a decade, I would have become aware of a cabin here. I continued my stalk.

As I lurked no more than forty yards distant from the lodge, a voice interrupted the silence—a booming voice, angry in tone, though clearly not directed toward me. I considered, then, retracing my steps and hurrying home, but curiosity and, I suppose, some sense of intrigue kept me glued to my post as I watched and listened.

Again came the bellowing voice from within the cabin, even louder than before. The accent was clearly French, yet, strain as I might, I could not make out the man's words. I stepped closer, soon finding myself on the narrow porch along the front of the cottage. The words of the angry man were now quite audible, and I realized he was not talking to himself. No, he spoke to someone else there with him.

"You!" he shouted. "You caused this! It is your doing and yours alone! Now, I have to live with this. I have to bear the burden of recalling this dark thing for the rest of my days. You get off easy. I am the one who must shoulder the shame, bear the constant grief."

Unable to tolerate the suspense, I peeked through the window pane. There, to my utter horror, pale in the glow of the oil lamp, lay a lifeless, denuded man, filleted wide like a whitefish on the cutting bench at the cannery. Seated near him, knife in hand, was a large man, sleeves rolled up and blood beyond his elbows.

"You, *mon frère*! You deserved death!"

Shuddering from fear and almost retching my last meal, I turned to run, tripping on the wooden steps. Scrambling to my feet, I bolted for the woods, falling again, not knowing if my hasty actions had alerted the man with the booming voice and bloody knife. I stumbled rather aimlessly in the dark, hoping to distance myself from the gory scene. After falling several times more, I took to crawling through the woods on hands and knees, praying to God Almighty I was heading in the best direction.

I heard the door open.

"Who is there?" came a bellow from behind me.

I froze, holding my breath, trembling in the silence.

"Show yourself, *mon ami*!"

In that dark, chilly blackness, I remained still as a tombstone for what seemed an eternity. Finally, I heard footsteps on the porch, followed by the slamming of the door. The warm glow of the oil lamp disappeared and, with no light to guide me, I recommenced crawling aimlessly through the woods, hoping to not circle back to the cabin, now as black as the rest of the forest. I realized my steady, slow crawl was well directed when my left hand landed on something soft—my watch cap! Yes! In minutes, I crawled onto my familiar trail and made my way not home, but to the house of the constable in La Pointe.

After nine days and as many sleepless nights, nights filled with fear and anxiety, a knock came on my door. Shotgun at the ready, I tripped the lock and stepped back, prepared to fire. To my utter relief, it was the constable, accompanied by the county sheriff. They'd found human remains—but not the remains I had earlier described to them.

Said the sheriff, "There's no doubt in my mind that the few burnt bones we found have been out there for a century. Maybe more. Looks like there was once a cabin but the signs tell me it burnt up as well. Most likely about the same time. What little is left is far too scorched and decayed to know just what happened there." He rubbed his chin. "I heard of a fellow long, long ago—a fur trapper—who took his own life after confessing to the murder of his brother. But, like I say, that was near a hundred years back. You couldn't have seen what you said you saw. And if you did, well, I sure don't know what you been drinkin', friend, but you might want to try something not so strong." He turned toward the door, then turned again. "And, if I was you, I would not be greetin' folks with a double-barrel shotgun in hand. 'Tain't a neighbor-like way to behave—least not here on the island."

With that, the constable and sheriff left. And, although I no longer fear for my life from the big Frenchman with the booming voice and bloody knife, I must admit, I have other fears—especially when I return from work along the back trail from La Pointe on moonless nights such as tonight.

END

James Brakken writes from his home in Wisconsin's Bayfield County. His novel, *The Treasure of Namakagon*, features a boy in an 1883 northern Wisconsin lumber camp and a legendary lost silver mine. The suspicious 1886 death of Chief Namaka-gon and the 1846 disappearance of a murder fugitive led to two more in the award-winning Chief Namakagon trilogy.

Brakken's writing won the Lake Superior Writers Award and the Wisconsin Writers Association's Jade Ring Award. His current project is *The Annotated Early Life Among the Indians*, the 1892 memoir of Madeline Island hero Benjamin Armstrong.

Brakken's books are available at BadgerValley.com and select outlets.

Superior Mordant

Judy Budreau

mordant *(adj.) caustic, biting commentary; (noun) fixative for dyeing natural fibers—Copper sulfate, for example, "saddens," turning colors toward the blue-green spectrum.*

Somewhere in the years before my grandma was killed by a drunk driver, in the years when we were sure cancer or chemotherapy were going to kill her, I said once at Sunday dinner that I didn't mind that my boyfriend often drove after having a few drinks. I told them that Jared said he felt more alert, that his senses were sharpened, and so he was a more careful, more deliberate driver.

Well. You'd think I had said that Jared was a mass murderer and that was okay by me. Uncle Ted started a lecture about underage drinking and Aunt Sally chimed in on irresponsible teenagers. All of it sounded a lot like every week's Sunday dinner, whenever I brought up any of the things I was thinking in those days.

Now Gram is gone, and the people who bought her house tore off the back porch and added a room even bigger than the house itself, with a second story that faces the lake, and probably has views of Lake Superior worth the price they paid. You can still see, in the fall and winter when enough trees are bare, even from fifty miles per hour on the Old Scenic, the tall stone chimney on the side of the house facing the driveway. The new people have a bunch of bikes leaning against the back of the house, some of them small enough for children. I hope the kids who live there now spend as much time as we did throwing rocks into the lake, giving back to the lake a small quota of what every storm and every season leaves on the beach.

I was always eager to finish those Sunday meals so I could wander up and down Gram's beach to search for rocks to save, and rocks to throw. I'd come to expect a short and dismissive discussion whenever I mentioned a topic of interest to me, but that week they really took off on the subject. When Aunt Sally was done with the chorus of Uncle Ted's lecture, my mom pointed to the view of Lake Superior out the dining room window.

"Laura, you've grown up believing that Lake Superior is the most dangerous thing in your world. But it isn't." She shook her head angrily. "It isn't."

I thought to myself, *Might be true. Probably is.* When you live within sight of a really large body of water, it becomes the reference point for everything else. Lake Superior is big, and big things happen on it, and because of it. The *Fitzgerald*. The *Mataafa*, and Split Rock Lighthouse. The thousand-foot lakers and salties that plied the harbor from March through December, and carried goods and jobs I dimly understood. But I knew even then that small things happen there, too, and I was just beginning to think about those, and finding I had to push against some of my family's big ideas to do it.

My brother David, who I know for a fact spent his college years with a constantly replenished six-pack in the back seat of the car my parents bought for him, shook his head and ruffled his boys' hair, one on each side of him.

"Laura, Laura, how are we supposed to raise responsible citizens with you spouting nonsense like that?"

My sister-in-law had that tight smile that meant her kids would not have the appallingly lax upbringing my brother and I had. Julie married David when he was finishing his Ph.D. and lived in a small apartment in Minneapolis that stank of benzene and acetone, the processes in his lab brought home on his clothing and his backpack. Julie was thrilled when he accepted a job with the University of Minnesota, until she found out it was with University of Minnesota–Duluth, a lesser campus, and she'd have to actually live in Duluth. Ten years later, she still showed no signs of wanting to be here, or wanting to be from here. At the moment, her sons were busy seeing which one of them could stuff the most carrots in his mouth. Which I thought my nephews would have done even if they lived in a Twin Cities suburb.

So, carrots and eye-rolling, and a lecture winding down, and the good mood at the table had disappeared. But my grandma—my Gram—all she said was, "Oh, honey. There are lots of things that sharpen our senses. Alcohol isn't one of them."

Then she leaned on the table to stand up, her signal that the dinner and the conversation were over.

She smiled at me and said, "Help me clear the table."

While Gram and I did the dishes, the family did the stuff they always did before leaving Gram's—my mom double-checked the daily meds lined up in Gram's little compartmented box, Aunt Sally folded some laundry, David and Uncle Ted oiled a squeaky door. The nephews wandered down to the lake to throw a few more rocks at each other or into the lake. I used three of Gram's dish-towels to dry the glasses, then the silverware, then the china plates and the pottery serving bowls. Each time I came to the drawer by the sink to get another towel, I waited for her to say more about the conversation at the dinner table.

Finally, she sat down at the kitchen table and said she'd rest while I tackled the pots from the stove. I left them to soak in the sink, and sat down across from her.

"Gram, was I wrong?"

"It's never wrong to say what you think, Laura," she said. "But what you think may not be right. I've found, in fact, that what I think is seldom the only, or the right way, to think."

She smiled her Gram-smile at me. "Maybe you'll find it's the same for you."

* * *

When Gram got sick, she wrote out a favorite quote— *When all is uncertain, everything is possible.* She wrote it several times, in different colors of ink, on pieces of handmade paper that her friend Ellen gave her. She taped them all over her house, one in each room, and used one as a book-mark. She taped one to the dashboard of her car so she would see it on the way to every doctor's appointment and every chemo treatment. When Ellen started driving her to most of her appointments, she made one for Ellen's car, too.

After the accident, when my mom and I followed the police car across the hill to St. Mary's, I kept thinking about those pieces of paper. Gram's favorites were blue—dyed linen-and-mulberry paper that Ellen made with indigo. For two or three years in the summer, Ellen used Gramps's old fish-cleaning shed down by the lake as her dye laboratory. I stayed away on fiber days, with wool and linen yarns soaking in stinking mordant baths. ("Copper sulfate is a superior mordant," said Ellen.) But if it was a paper day, especially an indigo paper day, I was in. I helped haul water up from the lake to mix the dye, and learned to stir it slowly with a thick wooden stick, gently so that no bubbles formed. We dipped the sheets of paper into the dye, then hung them between birch trees on lengths of twine. The dipped paper was an ugly, muddy yellow until it began to dry in the open air and we saw the iridescent greens, the subtle shades of blue. As the day wore on and the powerful dye lost some of its intensity, the color became lighter. By twilight, she was pulling paper the color of the darkening sky, that soft gray-purple blue we only see over great bodies of water.

On other days, Ellen used goldenrod and rhubarb for yellows and raspberry bark and leaves for pinks. Ugly, mud-colored water in those five-gallon buckets with barely a hint of color. With every dye bucket, Ellen experimented with different additions, hanging dark, wet papers to dry into softened pastel shades. Sometimes a reddish bucket produced pale tan papers. Other times, a brown bucket produced lavender. You think you're going to get one thing, and then you get another. It was that surprise that made the papers pretty to me. When I told Ellen that I liked these small surprises, she nodded.

"Beauty is just time working on ugly."

That is what I was thinking about when we saw Ellen in the emergency room, her arm in a sling and her face red and puffy with tears.

"I'm so sorry. I'm so sorry. I didn't see him coming," she sobbed as she fell into my mom's hug.

"I'm glad you are safe," said my mom. "I'm glad it wasn't worse."

Ellen reached out her good arm to me and drew me close. I let her cry on my head. Then someone came and asked my mom to come down the hall, and then she was back in the little exam room with me and Ellen and her face was white, her eyes red. And then it was time to go. We drove Ellen home to get her cat, and we brought them home with us and settled them in David's old room, and my mom asked me if I wanted a cup of cocoa. I said no and went to bed and fell asleep.

* * *

"I don't care," was the first thing I heard in the morning, my mother's voice raised in the kitchen. "I'm not going to bury her until I see the person who killed her. I want to look him in the eye, and I want him to know what he's done."

I walked into the kitchen to find my brother standing in his coat, talking to my mom's back as she stood at the sink.

"Well, Mom, we can delay the service, I guess. But we'll need to talk with the funeral home today."

"Okay, yes." I heard her take a deep breath. "So I'll call and take care of that. But we're not going to say good-bye to her until I see the man who took her life." My mom did not turn from the sink.

"He's seventeen, Mom." I saw my mother's back stiffen, her hands gripped the edge of the counter harder.

"Seventeen." Her voice was dull. When she turned to David, her face was hard. "Please see what you can find out from the sheriff's office. I want to see that boy before I say goodbye to your grandmother."

So David went off to see what he could find out, and Mom called the funeral home in Duluth where they'd taken Gram after we left the hospital.

* * *

Before this most recent chemo drug was available, Gram asked the family to meet with a hospice team from St. Mary's in case she decided to stop treatment. A nice woman around my mom's age, I think she was a social worker, came to Gram's house one Saturday morning. I went mostly because my mom started to cry when I said I didn't want to. David came without Julie or the boys, and Aunt Sally and Uncle Ted drove down from Two Harbors. We all sat in Gram's living room, and Gram sat in her favorite chair by the window, so every time I looked at her, I was also seeing the light on the lake, and the bright colors outside. Gram was a paler version of herself against all that light and color; she was already starting to disappear. But her smile and her voice were the same as the hospice lady helped her explain what she wanted if this were her final year of life. She wanted to stay home as long as possible, wanted to be surrounded by her favorite and familiar things—photographs, books, the quilt on the back of the sofa, the watercolor framed above the fireplace. She wanted to work in her garden, wanted to read in her favorite chairs inside and outside, wanted to be cremated and her ashes scattered on the lake like we'd done with Gramps's.

We all knew, but nobody said out loud, that she probably wouldn't be here much longer. A year was a substantial chunk of time to me at that age. To someone with Gram's decades, it must have seemed a too-small portion. I thought it was a pretty good day, as family days go, and we had cake at the end. The hospice lady stayed to help clean up the kitchen.

As it turned out, Gram's doctor encouraged her to try a new chemo drug, and she agreed. I think she wanted another season in her garden. But she was so tired, all she could manage that summer was to sit in the old metal chairs near the birch trees and look at the lake. By fall, she didn't want to make the effort to go outside. That's when the Sunday dinners became an every week thing, instead of a haphazard once or twice each month. We played cards around Gram's big dining room table, or sometimes Yahtzee.

One day during the week she died, only of course we didn't know it was the week she would die, I helped her sort through stuff in her sewing room. She handed me a small needle case that Gramps made for her from a piece of birch that fell near the lake. It was a perfect cylinder, with a neatly fitting cap, with Gramps's precise carving along the edge of the cap. On the cylinder, he'd carved Gram's initials.

Gram handed it to me. "If you could, honey, just keep aside some of my ashes. I'd like you to put them in the garden. On the coneflowers and black-eyed Susans, in the sun."

"Gram! I thought you were giving me this to keep after you're gone. In case I ever learn to sew."

"Oh, well, sure, you could use it for needles after that. Or whatever you like."

She pressed a small piece of Ellen's paper into my hand, pale blue and printed in Gram's carefully shaky handwriting: *when all is uncertain, everything is possible.*

"You'd better take one of these, too." I rubbed my thumb over the texture of the handmade paper, then put it in my pocket with the wooden cylinder. We went on sorting pieces of fabric, and buttons and patterns and about a thousand spools of thread.

* * *

Gram's funeral service was at the church she and Gramps went to all their married life, the church my mom and Uncle Ted had attended every Sunday while they lived under their parents' roof, and very few Sundays since. I knew it from Christmases and Easters and the church picnic in June and the craft bazaar the first weekend of hunting season. It didn't matter that very few people in the congregation knew us. They knew Gram, and they came by the carload to the visitation before the service, spoke movingly about her as we sat in the hard wooden pews and then on folding chairs in the church basement. We heard nice stories, and funny stories, and I even heard new stories about Gramps. A few times, someone began to mention the accident, or the boy who caused it, and my mom's expression hardened and she said, "Not here. Not here."

Then someone would bring us a new plate of potato salad and ham and fruit cocktail mixed with marshmallows and coconut and Cool Whip. Ellen made sure I had plenty of brownies and the bars with butterscotch chips and the bars with oatmeal crumble on top. Then it was time to go home.

That night, Mom decided that we'd all say goodbye to Gram on Monday and scatter her ashes, right after the court hearing for the boy who killed her. There was some tense conversation about this in the living room at Gram's house, Gram herself resting on the mantle in the cardboard box from the funeral home. After the kind of lengthy discussion my family could trademark, it was clear that nothing would sway my mother from the courthouse.

So on Monday morning, we drove to the St. Louis County courthouse, about midway up the hill that surrounds Duluth. Its wide steps ran down to a view of the harbor, with a weighty wall of granite behind it. A deputy explained to my mom that the family could write victim-impact statements to be read at the trial. For this initial hearing, no one from the public would be allowed to speak.

My mom argued with him. Red-faced, she said firmly, "I want to look him in the eye. I want him to know the pain he has caused."

"Sorry, ma'am. Not possible. You can take a seat over there."

David and Julie guided her to the row of chairs along the side of the room the deputy had pointed us to. Uncle Ted and Aunt Sally followed. Ellen sidled in next, cradling her broken arm. I sat down next to her. I looked at the boy, slumped in the chair next to his attorney, his parents sitting behind him staring straight ahead at the judge's bench. In that crowded and confusing room, I felt the buzz of anger, sure and strong. My mother's anger. My family's. Even gentle Ellen's. The kid's parents radiated anger and bewilderment at him, at everyone. The judge, in her black robe, looked tired and disgusted. But the kid—that kid—was a mirror, casting back to me the frightened uncertainty I felt it in every part of me, in my belly and my aching jaw and clenched fingers, in the dark behind my eyes.

The kid had to stand up and answer the judge's questions, and then the judge had the kid and the attorneys stand in front of her and we couldn't hear most of what they said. When the kid turned around, he was crying, and then everyone was leaving the courtroom and I was standing in that wide stone hallway and I was crying, too.

* * *

When we got back to Gram's house, the wind had shifted over the lake, and most of us went looking for warmer clothing. In the privacy of Gram's sewing room, I pulled on my jeans and an old sweatshirt. I wrapped the little slip of Ellen's gray-blue paper around the needle case, put them in my pocket, and headed downstairs.

Gram's ashes were on the mantle, still in the sturdy cardboard box from the funeral home because Uncle Ted wasn't done carving the walnut urn he started making when Gram got really sick. He apologized again, and we all said it was okay, maybe he should use it for something else when he finished, like his pipe tobacco. We were going to take the cardboard box down to the shore, but then Ellen looked inside and discovered that Gram was in a plastic bag inside the cardboard box. I was glad she'd looked, because while I think Gram would have been fine with going down to the lake in cardboard, I didn't think she'd like being carried there in a plastic bag with a twist tie. So then there was a flurry of discussion about what to do.

"A vase," said my mom. "I should look for a vase." But then she just stood there.

David suggested the giant tomato can on the shelf over the back door, the one where Gram kept years of spare keys, extra screws, and nails. I reached for it, emptied the keys and bits of hardware onto the kitchen counter and handed it to my brother. Julie had that tight smile again, the one that said she wasn't really part of this family. But she put on her coat and helped Aunt Sally and Uncle Ted with theirs and corralled her boys to go down to the lake.

David got Gramps's old rubber boots from the shed and put them on. I carried Gram in the tomato can down to the lake and stood with her for a minute looking at the late afternoon October sun on the water. Then I handed the can to David, and he waded in and dunked the can under the water. The ashes were heavy, and he had to shake and dip the can to get everything out. We all watched the water as the ashes dispersed, some of them blending with the waves and some settling into the cobbles in the shallow water. Mom reached down and sort of patted the water and then wiped her hand on her coat. She linked one of her arms through Ellen's good arm, and they turned toward the house. Aunt Sally and Uncle Ted each dipped a finger into the lake, and walked behind Ellen and Mom. The nephews were farther down the beach, flinging water on each other, squealing and running and dashing back to the water's edge. Julie sighed and started toward them.

David waded out of the lake and said he'd put the can and the boots away. As he passed me, he put his hand on my shoulder and squeezed, and I smiled at him. I was about to follow him when I remembered the needle case in my pocket. I'd forgotten to save some of Gram's ashes for the garden, her last request of me.

I stood looking at the lake, feeling that boundless, sad uncertainty. I found Ellen's pale blue paper in my pocket, and held it up to the pale blue sky. I opened my fingers and let the wind carry Gram's writing along the shore . . . *everything is possible*. Then I took off my socks and shoes and waded in. My bare feet touched the cold, round stones and the icy water closed over my shin bones, bit my fingers as I lowered the little wooden case to fill it. Some pain we are meant to feel.

END

Judy Budreau is a writer and teacher. Her work includes thirty years of helping people tell their stories, and her writing appears in a variety of regional and national media, as well as obscure literary journals. She lives in Duluth, Minnesota, with her partner, a scientist—he is certain that physics explains the world; she is fairly sure it's poetry. They have interesting dinner conversations. Learn more at www.judybudreau.com.